Cord

TONY,
ALL THE BEST TC YU-
Jay Beck

Jay Beck

Cordray's Mill

Table of Contents

Foreword

Cordray's Mill is a short work of fiction, set in a real place that is part of my childhood and is located about five miles from my grandmother Beck's home. My family usually stopped there when traveling to visit her, so I could have a ritual drink of the well water flowing from an open pipe. My father supervised the rebuilding of his family home in the late 1930s, as described in chapter two. The story, set in the late 1950s, was a time of many changes in the United States. I have used historical events from those years as a backdrop to tell a story that reflects many of my childhood memories repackaged into this fiction. The historical references to Korea, Vietnam and Civil Rights were as I experienced them or remembered them from my childhood.

My father worked in the Cordray's Mill for fifty cents a day when he was a boy at the lake, where I fished with him when I was a boy. I remember the stories of my parents dancing to an orchestra in the pavilion there when they were young, and in one of their love letters I discovered that is where they made love for the first time. I danced there with high school friends to a jukebox as a teenager. The descriptions of other places and events, such as the SOWEGA fair and the movie "Goodbye My Lady", are as I remembered them as a child and young man.

The names of people in the story, although not their demeanor, are largely taken from my family. Sam Lloyd's character was based on a man who worked for my grandparents in Atlanta. The story he tells John's kids, Graham and Wallace, was the story Sam told to me and my cousin, Henry.

Although I've tried to combine many events, ideas and sentiments from my life into the story, at its core, it is about family. Family is the thing we cling to in times of trouble and uncertainty. Family is what gets us through the hard times and what gives us the memories of the good. Family is not only about blood relatives, it is about those we choose to invite into our tent. It is about the ways we choose to love.

Mill house – Water wheel on the left of the mill house structure in the photo.

I am grateful for Rosalind Thomas, Martha Hall and Letty DuVall for reading and making suggestions for earlier versions of the manuscript.

About The Author

Jay Beck is a marketing and communications veteran and political consultant. He worked in the executive office of the President under Jimmy Carter and is a decorated Vietnam veteran with experience in finance, sports, and government, as well as many political campaigns, both domestic and international. He is the author of six novels.

For more, see: jaybeck.net

Introduction

Graham's father told him the story when he was dying in the hospital and when it was too late. Now he had no one left to share it with. He shook his head at the irony and tightened his grip on the steering wheel. Wasn't that supposed to be the point of stories? You needed to share them with others, like family or close friends who had similar experiences. The same stories were meant to be remembered and told again and again, with yet another beer and slight embellishments.

His story, this story, however, was the one he had never been able to share - not with friends, not with family. This story was dangerous to share. It was, however, the story that had driven his family for most of his life. It had wrecked the lives of almost everyone that he loved. It had directed him to be at this particular place and point in time and had put him on this bumpy road, driving down through the kudzu laden trees lining the sides of a Georgia highway, headed to what was left of Cordray's Mill. Like so many sad stories, it started with a woman.

The Trip

The doctors could do nothing to save Rhonda. She was lying in agony on the white metal bed in a Boston hospital room. There was the smell of disinfectant, there was the painful swelling, and there was the blood, and they were all one and the same. Cleo Mansfield leaned over, murmuring as she held her friend's hand and watched her struggle to work for each breath.

Lying there, in addition to the waves of pain, Rhonda felt the increasing discomfort of emotional pressure to talk before the police arrived. Her face contorted as she drew in the air and struggled to speak through her swollen lips and a broken nose.

"At first, when he gave me the bag that's been down there, I didn't know what was in it." She labored to prepare for the next sentence. "Later, when he told me, he said, it was supposed to stay hidden in the basement till they could spend it and not get caught." She grabbed tighter to Cleo's hand. "When those others found out, they made him talk and then came for me."

Feeling a chill up her back. Cleo probed. "What are you talking about? What? They beat you up and did this to you, over that luggage?"

Rhonda shook her head back and forth. "They didn't know for sure I had it. Once they started, they just kept beating on me. I woulda told them, but I kept passing out and then that fella started in on me with the knife."

A nurse came in, interrupting the conversation and checked Rhonda's vitals. She changed the bandages, which continued to be soaked with blood, to fresh dry ones. She also ran her hands over the swelling protruding from Rhonda's face, arms, and stomach. Then she looked at the chart and shook her head. "Honey, you're the first lady I've ever seen with hemophilia." She frowned at the suffering woman and tapped the chart. "Didn't you know you had it? Didn't you tell those folks not to hit and cut you like this?" The nurse looked at Cleo and pointed to the bed. "Why, didn't she tell them? Everybody has heard about that Russian prince who had it and was killed by the communists. I mean, it's 1957 already!" She pumped the blood pressure machine strapped to the woman's arm and looked at the results, frowning. "Mmmm."

Rhonda, taking shallow yet painful breaths, turned to the nurse, "Can you give me something for the pain?"

The nurse wrote something on her chart and tapped it again with the pen. She was doing her job. "Sorry, hon. Nothing stronger than what we have given you already, unless your doctor orders it." She sniffed.

Cleo lashed out at the nurse, walking quickly over to her and using her height advantage to add intimidation, "She doesn't have a doctor, lady. We don't have any money for doctors." The nurse's face blanched, and she stepped back, nodding. She held the chart attached to the clipboard over her chest protectively as Cleo continued, "Whoever they assigned to her when she was brought in has not been around. Can't you call someone? Give her something, for God's sake!"

The nurse nervously edged sideways to the door. "Sorry. I'm doing all I can. She's in tough shape. I'm not sure-"

Cleo gave the woman a quick look of disgust and dismissal. She was good at that. Not only did she have a beautiful face, but she also knew how to give it a serious, daunting look. She had learned quickly how to survive in the bar where they both were employed. She chose the clothes that would get her noticed, get her tips, and help her make the best living she could, but that was also the trap. That was the two-edged sword. Cleo had to learn to handle all those side looks, innuendos, grabbing's, sneers, barely whispered words behind her back and others in her face. Working the bar taught her how to control her self-assured confidence. She could present an irresistible interest or a gut-chilling caution to whatever she had to say. She sniffed at the nurse, "Then just leave us in peace," and turned to Rhonda, who was squeezing her eyes in pain.

After the wave of pain passed, Rhonda looked at her friend and reached again to touch her hand. "Cleo, honey, once those men, those robbers, find out you are my roommate, they'll come after you, for sure. They'll hurt you. They'll find the money."

Cleo took a deep breath to calm the chill that ran up her back. She also controlled her impulse to roll her eyes in exasperation. Rhonda's desperate needs where men were involved and her inability to say "no" to handsy customers had gotten them into this situation. Cleo knew better. It had not taken her too many mornings waking up with stale sweat and midnight regret to understand the empty promises of the big talkers. She leaned toward her housemate. "Why didn't you tell me about all this? Maybe I could have helped. What is it with the suitcase?"

Rhonda just looked at her, "Honey, when you do a favor for a man, make sure he's a boyfriend worth having. He never told me before that he was in on the robbery." Her head pressed back in pain on the thin pillow as she caught her breath. "You got to get out. All those men who ain't got caught already have gone crazy. Turning on each other. They'll be coming for you next." She shook her head from side to side. "It don't matter that you don't know anything about the robbery. They can't take the risk that you might talk. The money they took is in that suitcase. When they figure you know me, that's all they'll need to come for you to see if you got it. Pack your stuff. Get that special suitcase and take it. It's in the back of the storage unit in the cellar under a tarp. Hurry and run. Run where they can't find you."

Another chill went through Cleo. Rhonda had been so desperate for a man to define her; she'd chosen anyone who paid her attention. It was that need that would soon kill her. It was time for Cleo to cut the cord. It would do her no good to still be there when the police arrived. Even worse, the robbers, who beat Rhonda and would soon be after her, might show up.

As soon as Rhonda drifted off to sleep, she left. She knew the man who had been Rhonda's boyfriend and had seen him with some of the others. Sometimes when they drank a lot, they implied things, and afterward, the women in the bar talked about it, speculating but not really believing. She never really thought it could have been THAT.

Where could she go? The people who had beaten Rhonda had deep ties to the rough edge of society. My God, here was her friend talking about ... she was confirming that those were the men who had stuck up the damn Brinks warehouse. She had to go away where they would never think to look for her. Her mind raced over the possibilities, thinking and discarding. Suddenly, she remembered a friend she had made two years earlier in the bar. They had hung out for a time, laughing and swapping stories. The vivacious young college girl from Georgia had told her of life down there in that remote and primitive state. She told her that she had left because it was in the middle of nowhere and there was nothing to do down there.

She reached the apartment after a quick stop to explain her absence from the bar and draw out all the money she had from the bank. Inside, it was still a mess. Next to the spot where there was overturned furniture and some broken dishes, she could see the blood still on the floor from where Rhonda had been beaten. Hurriedly. she searched through her address book and found the number, which she then dialed. "Is this Wembley dorm? Can I speak to Annie Mills?" As she waited, she tried to gain control over her emotions. *Okay, be patient and positive. Be glad to hear her voice.* Standing there and holding the phone in the hallway nook, she looked around the apartment and thought about what she needed to take with her.

Then finally, on the line, she heard the expectant drawl of privilege asking who was calling and responded, "Annie! This is Cleo Mansfield."

Immediately, Annie Mills took over the conversation and was effusive in telling Cleo about her latest Harvard boyfriend. Cleo let her ramble for a few minutes because she dared not interrupt the young girl. Finally, Annie asked Cleo about her life. Cleo, who had been impatiently waiting for the younger Annie to finish, had no trouble in letting her voice express her concern. "I've been okay, but something bad has come up. I really need your help." Oblivious, Annie continued to ramble and interject personal stories of her life at college and in the dorm. Cleo struggled to manage her patience and redirect the conversation.

She let her voice whine in fear when she said, "You may be the only friend I can count on." Another whine. "Please. You remember telling me about your grandmother who lives down in that small Georgia town?" Finally getting the young woman's full attention, she was able to give Annie a prepared story about being in an abusive relationship that had become dangerous. She said that the rough man was stalking her and had already hurt her once. Cleo told her that she needed to escape Boston and go somewhere "this maniac" could not find her.

She worked the conversation to ask about Annie's grandmother and the guest house in the backyard Annie had mentioned, and Annie said, "Yeah. If you go down there to Cordray's Mill where my grandmother lives, you can hide where no one will ever find you. But listen Cleo, I've gotta warn you, you'll be bored to death. Nothing down there but woods 'n water." Finally, after embellishing the danger and at Cleo's continued insistence, Annie called her grandmother, then immediately called Cleo back. The trip was on.

Hurry.

She jammed her clothes into two bags and looked around the apartment to see if she had forgotten anything she needed. Whatever was left, those crooks were welcome to have. Then she dragged out the heavier big piece of luggage from the cellar that was in her roommate's storage cubby. She knew that US Highway 1 was the major route south, so she filled up the gas, wheeled her old car onto the highway, and headed toward the unknown wilds of South Georgia.

As she cleared the Boston city limits, Cleo began to relax and noticed the crusty sweat of dried fear on her. She gripped the steering wheel tightly as she navigated around the big trucks hogging the road. She watched the rear-view mirror, looking to see if maybe the same car might be following behind her. Concentrating, she managed to hold her bladder until she got to New York.

She felt certain that it was most important to keep her whereabouts a secret from anyone else she knew in Boston. That meant a small town and a low profile. According to Annie Mills, there was no place that fit those requirements better than Cordray's Mill. That meant she would be lonely. She also needed to keep the grandmother from getting too nosey and comparing notes with Annie back in Boston. From what Annie had told her, they didn't talk or write too often. If she could get on the good side of the grandmother, maybe she would trust her and not check up on her background too much. She would also need to keep the frivolous Annie from asking too many questions, but the granddaughter seemed only interested in her own social life. Cleo felt that if she sent Annie an occasional, short, cheerful letter, that should take care of her. When she crossed the Susquehanna River, she saw a sign for lodging in the small town of Darlington, Maryland. There, she found an inn where she slept for twelve hours.

The next morning, she was still exhausted and frightened. By the time she had reoriented herself to the tasks she had ahead of her, it was noon. The one thing this long trip had given her was time to think. At a roadside grocery store, she bought some food she could use to make sandwiches on the side of the highway. Now, free from the intimidation and paranoia she had felt in Boston, she planned her next moves. She needed some clothes for the warmer climate of South Georgia, and after looking at a gas station map, she decided to stop in Charlotte, North Carolina, to do some shopping.

Money. The cash she withdrew from her bank account was hardly enough to get her to Georgia Tonight, she would look in the suitcase and, assuming there was money in it, she would take some to live on. She wondered how much there was, and if it was all money or some jewelry or other goodies. Who knew how much the boyfriend had removed? She could count it tonight but would have to be careful no one sees her. Trust no one.

After another long day of driving and being careful to stay under the speed limit, she found another out-of-the-way small hotel just off the highway near Richmond. First, she brought in her personal luggage into her hotel room. She needed to go through the bags carefully and reorganize them according to what she really had to use. It took a separate trip out to the car just to lug that monster bag. The big, wide suitcase that Rhonda had been hiding for her boyfriend was heavier than she remembered. It must have been the adrenalin rushing through her that had helped her before when she had dragged it up from the apartment storage area and out to her car.

She locked the door to her rented room and then pushed a chair up against the door handle. Windows all down, shut, and secure. Now to the suitcase. Click. Click. Open.

There was nothing in it but money. The sight took her breath away. It was like all that cash swelled upwards when she lifted the lid. She had to go across the room and sit in a chair just to look at it for a while. This stash was not just a few hundred or a few thousand dollars from some small-time con or stick-up. The Brinks job had been a major theft. It looked to be a mixture of $20s and $100s and but there were also some $10s and $5s. A lot of it was wrapped inside small paper bags with the amount written in pencil on the outside, and some stacks were wrapped in rubber bands. Some of the rubber bands had broken, and the cash spilled out all over the place.

The papers in Boston had speculated that the Brinks depository robbery, which happened a few years ago, was almost three million dollars. It was the biggest robbery in U.S. history. What she had here looked like most of the loot. She thought, *Lord! You could buy a good house for $ 20,000.00. You could buy a hundred of those houses for what was here and still have enough left over to keep you living in style all your life.*

Cleo had to calm herself from shaking. This suitcase full of money was why Rhonda was beaten so badly. It was why the robbers would continue to look for her and come after her for as long as they were alive and not in jail. She remembered the callous demeanor of some of the associates of Rhonda's boyfriend from earlier in the bar where she worked. They must be the ones who would be looking for her. She was in much bigger trouble than she had imagined. Even worse, now that she had all this money with her, she was part of it.

How could she go to the police and just turn herself in? They would assume that she was in on the whole thing from the beginning. She was no longer innocent. No one would believe her. They would all be after her. Her looks which had always been her greatest asset, were now working against her. She was the looker who worked in a bar, the woman who was the roommate of the girlfriend of one of the criminals, the woman who had met some of the others in the gang, who lived in the building where the money was stashed in the cellar, who knew her roommate had an extra suitcase in the basement, the woman who had left town with the money, the woman whose roommate was, by now, likely dead. She was everyone's target, and with this much money involved, they would never stop looking for her. Her stomach was churning. She had to get ahold of herself.

Okay. She had already decided what she needed to do, and now all she had to do was follow through. She had set up her escape plan using Annie Mills and was already into it. She had crossed the line to becoming a thief. Now she had to plan way ahead, and not just about her leaving town for a few months. All that money in the heavy suitcase would direct her life from here on out. She sat there, looking at her future bulging over the top of the bag.

After she calmed down, she pulled out enough money to take care of her for the next several months, which would give her the time to decide what to do for the longer term. Now she had enough money with her to go to the fanciest women's clothing store in Charlotte the next day and get any clothes she might need for the warmer climate. She'd pay cash and leave town immediately. No one would catch her. She thought that the nice, new clothes would make her seem more upscale and acceptable to Annie's grandmother. She would look more like the blue bloods who went to her granddaughter's college. That way, Cleo would look like someone who would be a friend to the college girl, Annie Mills, not a woman who worked in a bar.

She allowed a feeling of satisfaction to roll over her. She checked herself out in the mirror, twisting left then right, testing a less fearful and more confident look. She found in there the face that would fit her new life as a regular citizen. She was smart enough to pull this off. Plus, she thought, as she put the bills into her purse and made a mental list for her shopping trip, that she had always wanted to have some really nice clothes for herself. She wanted clothes that were better than she had ever had before, like those she had seen worn in magazines and by the fancy woman on the streets of Boston. Later the next day, before she left the upscale apparel store carrying the bags strained with her new wardrobe, she looked again in the mirror and pulled down her dress to smooth out the wrinkles. She smiled at her new self and thought that at least she'd get all these fancy clothes out of it.

The Lighthouse

Joyce Cordray sat quietly in her living room, looking through the screen door out across the porch at the two-lane blacktop in front of her house, thinking about the past. She had been doing that a lot these days, remembering her husband, who had died a few years before. She recalled the stories of how her husband's family had developed this territory generations ago.

The Creek Indian Wars cleared the area of the native families who had, for a millennium, camped on the sides of the several tributaries up and down the corridor of the naturally sloping homestead. When the Indians were driven to the West 150 years ago, the white settlers of the Cordray family came to bring civilization to this patch of land.

They noticed the streams and drainage runoff that had crossed the former Indian trail for hundreds of years from the slightly higher tracts north of them. At the end of that thirty-mile stretch of long and fecund gully created by the Ichawaynochaway Creek, they saw an opportunity. At a narrow point in the flow, they built a dam. The barrier collected water in a thousand-yard-wide corridor from several locations to make the pond that now fed the wooden water wheel by the grist mill. Below the dam, the overflow burrowed into the soft loamy Georgia ground, creating marshy lowlands stretching southward, eventually joining the Flint River and into Florida. Inside the ninety-year-old mill, the force of the spinning wheel turned massive smooth flat round stones that scraped against each other to pulverize the grains of corn poured between them.

Joyce Cordray walked onto the porch to get a better look at the bridge spanning over the dam and the walkway that paralleled the road near the spillover. In addition to being a footpath, it was handy to untangle and remove tree limbs and other debris from the lip of the dam during the occasional flooding. A modest swimming pool of wood, made from treated railroad ties, was built later and filled with water from the lake. An open well on the side of the road with pouring water coming from a pipe offered an additional attraction for thirsty travelers. The area around the mill became a favorite place for picnics, swimming, and fishing, stretching north in a thousand-acre lake in front of the dam. The interior of the swimming pool was later covered in cement blocks as the wood began to rot.

A pavilion for dancing was added nearby as well as a small hotel. In the 1920s, a ten-piece orchestra played for dancers on a wooden dance floor covered with corn meal to make the dancing smoother. The hotel burned down in the 1930s. By the 1940s, most of the activity in the pavilion became square dancing and, later, with the help of a jukebox, rock and roll. The corn meal stayed. As roads got better and automobiles provided a more convenient form of transportation to places further away, the community of Cordray's Mill became less of an attraction as people searched for the new. This ongoing gradual decline in commerce was what worried Joyce Cordray as she watched the empty road from her front porch.

Across the street, the stillness around the swimming pool reminded her that it had been a while since she had gotten a call or letter from her daughter or her granddaughter. These days, she barely heard from anyone living more than ten miles away. She reentered the living room carefully with her cane, and looked along the wall at the photos of her family, taken when they last visited several years ago. A sad realization came over her that they might never return during her lifetime.

As she settled back down in her favorite inside chair, her dog, Talmadge, yawned and rolled over near her feet. She continued to reminisce about past years and happier times, which was also something she did more of, since nothing new or interesting was happening. She looked at the glass lamp beside her that had been converted from kerosene to electrical, and remembered the time years ago when they were upgrading the house and installed indoor plumbing and electricity for the first time.

During the construction, the Cordray family stayed over in the cottage that had been built either to be used as a guest house or for their daughter and her family in case they decided to move back home after she married. Watching the renovation of their home, both she and her husband had been impressed with the local workers who were unemployed because of the depression. Her husband had sketched the plans of what he wanted in the dirt by the house and pointed out the location of various rooms. He showed where the doors and windows would go and gave the measurements to a group of carpenters. The men watched in overalls with hammers dangling from the leg strap and Prince Albert chewing tobacco cans in some of their breast flap pockets.

He pointed out the places to avoid so as not to damage the big oak and pine trees scattered around the yard. Thinking of Joyce, he had also staked out a spot on the side to add some fruit trees, a vegetable garden, and even shrubs that would flower in the backyard sunlight.

After the final instructions the next morning, the small army of carpenters and helpers began to pull apart the old house piece by piece. The roof tiles were collected. Each window was stacked with the others. Each door frame was put in its place. Each nail was hammered straight after it had been pulled. When the new materials arrived on a flatbed truck from Albany, the two separate piles of building supplies were stacked side by side, awaiting re-assembly.

Then the rebuild started. Everyone watched carefully as a special man with experience came over from Albany to oversee the job with the plumbing and electrical wiring. These aspects of house building were new to most of the workers.

Bricks were laid around to sturdy the foundation. They set the posts and studs and began putting up the walls. Mostly they used the old materials, but occasionally – a piece of wood needed to be cut to fit a space in the new wall. The workers were so proficient that a builder could look at the empty gap, go away and cut the wood, and it would fit in the space tight enough to hold there, while the man went to look for the nails. Those were the days of real carpenters.

Layer by layer, the house was built from the ground up. Windows and doors were set in place. The stairway to the attic was put in, and the roof went on.

Day after day, the workmen showed up early and stayed late. The piles of the old house dwindled into the new. The new pieces of modern technology found their places. Paint was applied. Floors were sanded and shellacked. One morning, they all showed up and hauled the furniture out of several of the neighbor's barns and garages into the new house, to be placed according to Joyce Cordray's instructions.

Then, curtains were hung, rugs laid out, and dishes washed and put away. By late in the day, everything was done. Then they remembered the lights. Before this time, there were no electric lights in Cordray's Mill, even though a power cable had recently been hung on a row of poles out on the road leading to Morgan. Now the new house was attached to the power. In the years before, at night, everyone used kerosene lanterns and went to bed early. However, as this day turned to dusk and the summer dark settled in, they turned on the light in the living room.

Suddenly, the room burst into a bright and harsh glow from the one bulb suspended from a cord in the middle of the ceiling. Later they would add a shade over the bulb, but the first light was like a flash. Everything the light could see was illuminated, everything else was dark. The stuffed couch covered in a patterned cloth had almost faded in the contrast brightness, while when you looked behind it, it was so dark, you could not see much of anything along the wall.

From outside the house, there was a collective gasp. The workmen and those still admiring the finished product, now could see the Cordray family lit up like it was day. It felt like there was a movie going on in the living room, and everyone was watching. Then everyone ran out to see the glowing living room as it continued to get darker outside.

When someone looked away from the house, it took several moments for their eyes to re-adjust to the natural moonlight. Then there was this pull, this craving to look back again. There it was, still glowing. Her husband went back in and, one by one, turned on all the rest of the lights in the house.

Look, there's the bedroom. There's the kitchen. There goes the dining room. The house gradually became like a dollhouse in the center of an empty room. All around, everything else was dark except for a yellow glow coming through the curtains of some room.

Then, everyone came in for the experience of being in a lit room. They walked around, looking at their hands, bright towards the light and dark on the other side. They rubbed their eyes and squinted out the window, trying to see the other people and wondering what they looked like to those on the lawn while standing there in the bright house. Some would ask their daughter to stand by the window while they ran outside to look at her and the spot they had just vacated.

Soon the Cordrays became weary from the long day and began to turn out the lights and prepare for bed, all except the living room light. When that happened, the Cordrays could see through the windows, from the other darkened rooms, the faint images and feet of people still standing in the dark looking at their house. There, outside the circle of light from the living room, cigarettes glowed when inhaled, but the feet and legs up to the knee were the only parts they could see. The rest were in the shadows, looking in from the dark of the night. The next day, there was a pattern, a circle of footprints around the house, giving the distance, the measure of light.

Talmadge made a loud doggie woof from a dream which drew her out of her reverie. She was sad to leave those better times when she was younger. Now alone, she had to support herself from the rent the farmers paid her to use the nearby land that her husband's family had acquired over many years. Cordray's Mill was less than a village, on a road surrounded by woods and a dwindling collection of family farms. She thought to herself, that the pace of the world had become unkind. Each year, there seemed to be less leftover, and people tried to bargain her down for everything they paid; less and less. The world her family had built was going away. Then she realized that the phone was ringing. Talmadge, awakened from his slumber, stood up, stretched, and looked around. She picked up the phone, and it was her granddaughter from Boston. There was someone coming.

Arrival

Four nights later, Talmadge suddenly raised his head, batted his tail on the floor, and looked out through the screen door into the yard with suspicion. Joyce Cordray did not hear the motor stop or the car door shut, but when she answered a knock at her door, there was a tall, trim young woman, wet from the rain, shivering at her front door.

The woman huddled on the porch close to the house to avoid the downpour and introduced herself as the friend of her granddaughter, Annie, who she was expecting. After the introductions, Mrs. Cordray felt an immediate connection to the woman, yet still felt in her country caution that she needed to know a little more about this mystery guest. She left the screen door between them, hesitated, and rubbed the key to the guest house in her hand. She glanced out into the dark in the direction of the guest house as she slowly cracked the screen door. "I hope you'll be able to find everything all right? It's so late and raining and all, I don't feel like I'm doing much to welcome you." She felt that, somehow, the stranger understood her concern that being alone in this rural area was the reason for her probing.

The woman took a step back, nodding. "Yes ma'am. I'm … thank you. I'm sure it will be just fine." She smiled, bowed slightly, and began to turn toward the small house tucked away near the barn.

Mrs. Cordray, feeling that she needed to ask this stranger more before letting her go, spoke in a slightly elevated voice, "My Annie told me a little bit about what brought you down here. Let me get a good look at you in the light." She stepped back from blocking the light over the door. The glow fell on the face and form of the woman who, even wet with the rain, was strangely poised and self-contained. "Well, you are pretty." She raised her eyebrows. "No wonder the men folk noticed you."

The woman ducked her head in a humble motion. "Well, ma'am, it was just this one situation, and he was very ... aggressive, and frankly, it felt dangerous. He had this kind of fix on me, and a couple of times, it was all I could do to get away. He is very prominent and powerful, so I had to leave and go someplace where he couldn't find me." She paused, and there seemed to be the beginnings of tears forming in the corners of her eyes. "I'm afraid he will come looking for me or ... send some of the people he knows. Like I said, he is well-connected. I really need to lay low. Please don't say anything that will give me away."

Joyce Cordray thought, *Mmmmm.* There was something about her that showed a defiance, even though she tried to hide it. She could tell, even with her wet from the rain and disheveled from the trip, that this woman was more worldly and aggressive than the other people, particularly the local women she knew. Still, she could see this stranger seemed vulnerable and in need, and, after all, she was a friend of her granddaughter. Mrs. Cordray softened. "I'm so sorry, my dear. Annie didn't tell me it was this bad. I think she didn't want to upset me. She sometimes thinks I'm a helpless old lady. Don't worry. We'll look after you, and you can stay as long as you like." Talmadge had slowly made his way to the screen and sniffed at the stranger. Satisfied, she met his approval, he moved back into the room and lay back down on the rug.

The woman shivered and brushed the damp hair from her forehead. "I'm happy to pay my way, and I can do chores and help around here if you need me."

"That will be just fine." She pointed. "The house back there has been shut up for a spell, so it may be a little musty. I'll get John to take a look to make sure everything is running okay." She thought she needed to explain herself and added, "He is a widower with two young boys who live near here and is a fishing guide, but also helps me keep things straight." She gave another glance in the direction of the guesthouse.

Mrs. Cordray paused and thought for a moment, wondering if she had been clear or had confused this young woman. "Actually, he's not a widower, but might as well be. His wife left him and the boys." Mrs. Cordray stopped to ponder what she had just said as she looked into the night through the rainswept trees. No, she was making what she was trying to say even more confusing. She continued almost as though she was talking to herself. "There was something wrong with her. He's got to raise those sweet little boys by himself. It's not easy for him, so I try to get him jobs to help." She shook her head. "Lordy, here I am rambling, and you haven't even unpacked yet." She looked out at the car in the muddy driveway and said with slightly forced hospitality. "If you like, you can stay in here with me in my spare room for a few days, till you get the house settled."

The woman gave her a slight smile and a bow. "Thank you so much ma'am, but I think I'll go ahead and get to it if that's all right with you. Can I park my car in the barn you have out there? I want to be as inconspicuous as possible." She hesitated expectantly.

"Sure. Sure, honey. You just make yourself at home and come on back over here in the morning. I'll have some breakfast for you. We put some basic food over there in the other house, but you come on back over here for breakfast. I get up early, and there will be coffee on. The back door here will be open for you, so help yourself. If something is not working right, make a list, and we'll get John to fix it. We're not as backward around here as some people think. They've even got a television station over in Albany. We can't get it yet, but I've talked to people who have seen it. They send out pictures six or eight hours a day."

As they talked, she had been slowly moving further through the door onto the porch and held up the key to the guest house. "Here, I forgot to give you this."

Cleo took it respectfully, nodding. "Thank you, mam. I'll be very careful, and I sure do appreciate you helping me out. Please just don't make a big fuss to anyone about where I'm from."

Coffee with Cordray

During a mid-morning pause in the rain that had been steady for the past two days, Mrs. Cordray shouted out the back door and invited Cleo to join her in her living room for coffee and homemade cookies. Together now, in the light of day, she could see the young woman was even more attractive than she had thought the night before. Her lovely face was accented with bright green eyes and auburn hair that, when dry, bounced in full natural waves.

The rain soon continued in earnest, and the lake began to crest, edging into one side of Mrs. Cordray's yard. She had left her front door open to invite a cool breeze from the rain. A glance through the screen door showed little activity on Georgia State Route 45, called Bermuda Street, which carried the traffic from Albany to nearby Morgan. Once they settled into the living room, she pumped her guest for news of her granddaughter in Boston. She could feel Cleo's reluctance and was wondering if the stranger was protecting Annie for behaving in ways that she would not want her grandmother to learn. Or could it be that this woman and her granddaughter were not as close as they both had implied?

The slightly awkward conversation was interrupted when they heard splashing, and looked through the screen door to see a sixty-nine-year-old Sam Lloyd making an impressive run through the yard, weaving around the deepening puddles and onto the porch veranda.

He stopped by the wooden slat swing, held firm by a metal chain on either side, and stood with his hat off, waiting. Cleo stood to help Mrs. Cordray as she slowly pulled herself up. Then, she ambled to the door using her cane, leaving the screen between her and Sam.

He nodded respectfully as she approached. "Miss Cordray, the lake is pushing at the dam, and I'm thinking we should let off some more of that water to be safe. Radio says it might keep on raining for another day or two. That dam hasn't been fixed or tested in a long time, and I think it's better we might take the chance of losing a couple of days in the mill next week to low water, than let the dam break and be stuck for a long time and lots of money to fix it. I just want to ask your thoughts on that."

With her hand on the door panel, she leaned to look past him through the drizzle toward the bridge and mill on the other side. "I spec you're right. I think that's what my husband might have done."

"Yes'm."

Now she noticed his clothing for the first time. "You got soaking wet coming over here to see me. Want to come in for some coffee fore you go back? Or ... I could bring some to you out here?" She glanced back into the living room and then back to Sam. "Miss Cleo, that friend of my granddaughter I told you was coming, is visiting with me inside."

He leaned around Mrs. Cordray and nodded through the screen door into the dark living room at the figure standing behind her. "No ma'am. Pleased to meet you Miss Cleo, but I'd best be getting back to do the work. I'm sorry to interrupt your visit."

Mrs. Cordray slumped a little at the doorway. "Sam, you know you are never any trouble. Nowadays, you and John are responsible for almost everything around here. I don't know how I'd get on without you. I's just telling Miss Cleo," she turned to nod to her guest inside the room then back to Sam, "how much you have meant to me running the mill and being so kind after my husband passed."

He rolled the hat around in his hands, using the brim to complete the circle. To Cleo, the black man seemed overly respectful of the older lady. She could tell there was a friendly bond between them, but it seemed to have an edge of theater. "Yes mam." Then he nodded with a slight bow towards the dark interior of the room. "Miss Cleo, hope you have a pleasant stay, and I hope you and Mrs. Cordray are having a nice visit in all this rain."

Cleo stepped forward into the light to stand beside Mrs. Cordray. "Thank you, Sam. Nice to meet you also. You need to dry off and get on some dry clothes when you get back over to the mill. You'll catch a cold like that."

"Yes'm. I'll be careful." He nodded and bent slightly as he stepped back to leave. "You ladies be careful too when you walk out here on the slick wood and in the yard out there. You don't want to fall or nothin'." Cracks appeared on the sides of his face as he grinned and chuckled mostly to himself. "We don't want Miss Carolyn over at the store to have to call the ambulance on either of you two."

Mrs. Cordray let out a 'Ha'. "You know Sam, she's more likely gonna have to call it on you for falling in that water or catching your hand between those big mill stones. You be careful now."

He backed out into the rain and jogged back across the lawn toward the mill. As Mrs. Cordray was closing the door, she smiled at Cleo, "That Sam is the most reliable person I know."

Cleo, watching, said, "I thought you said he was almost seventy years old. He runs like a college athlete."

Mrs. Cordray smiled as she walked back into the center of the room. "You wouldn't believe it to see him 'cause he's not too tall and so thin and wiry, but he's very strong. A couple years back, John and some others nailed a pipe across some tree limbs to do some chin-ups and such. They were all pumped up at themselves at being able to do eight or ten chin-ups and playing in the yard when Sam walked by on some errand. Well, one of the other young men asked him if he wanted to try it." She smiled and leaned the cane she had been using almost absentmindedly against the side table. She let herself down in her chair with a sigh. "Well, he came over there and must have done twenty or more, before he stopped. He was not the least winded or tired. He just smiled and thanked them for the chance to try it. He's worked every day in his life, and it shows."

Cleo took another look across the yard toward the mill. "He's so deferential to you ... well, I guess ... to all of us who are white. I'm not used to that, being from Massachusetts."

Joyce Cordray followed her gaze outside at the yard. "Well, it's just a little different down here."

Cleo carefully picked up the coffee cups which rattled in the saucers and took them into the kitchen. She returned to pet Talmadge who had raised his head at her activity. "I need to get back over to the house. There is a window open that's kind of stuck, and I'm afraid the wind might be pushing some of that rain inside." She moved toward the back door.

Joyce Cordray smoothed her skirt. "Well come on back soon. I want to know more about my granddaughter and find out some more about what you were doing up there in Boston." She looked through the window at the cottage and thought to herself that she'd probably never get the full story about her granddaughter. "I'm glad to have you here. Sorry you had to come for an unpleasant reason, but it's sure nice to have the company."

On her way back into the small house, Cleo took advantage of another pause in the rain and stopped to finish unloading the car and then opened the barn doors to hide the car inside. She had taken out enough money from the suitcase to last her for what she estimated would be six months. She wondered if she should try to find a place to hide the rest of it, either in or under the guesthouse.

Once inside the barn, she looked around. Other than a section to the right where there were lawnmowers and some other frequently used yard tools, the barn was musty and dusty. There were leather mule collars and other tackle handing on pegs on the sidewalls that were crusty and rotting. Sections of the old dirt floor were so unused that there was a layer of dust, like a bleached grey powder from the lack of sunlight, and marked around the edges by conical doodlebug holes. There was plenty of space, and she drove the car inside. She found an old tarpaulin which she draped over it to keep off the dust and hide the Massachusetts tag from any prying eyes.

On the spur of the moment, she decided to bury the suitcase under a half-rotten piece of plywood, and some crumbly paper sacks over in a far corner that looked like no one had been there in years. Then, she carefully scattered the sand and dust over the pile to disguise that it had been disturbed. She gathered dust from the other side of the barn and poured it in a pattern left and right to cover her footprints leading to the corner where the suitcase was hidden. Satisfied that she had not left a trail and that the floor looked smooth and even, she was also glad to see it was dry everywhere, so the place felt safe. It would have to do for now. She closed the doors and turned the wooden handle on the outside to keep them shut.

Cleo and Carolyn

By the next morning, the rain had stopped. The noise of a car arriving, drew Cleo to her window to see a heavyset woman park across the road by the side of the country store with two gas pumps in the front, mounted in an oval of concrete. She noticed that the circular glass bubble on both pumps was cracked, and one side was missing most of the glass containing the company name. The woman was wearing a long shirt that bloomed about her with a brightly colored pattern, reaching down to partially conceal her hips and the full, dark skirt below. She could see there was some effort involved for the woman to climb the steps using the handrail before she steadied herself and then opened the door.

Cleo watched the lights flick on through the store windows, and a calico cat walked out to stretch and smell the wood flooring and the steps before finding a place to lie down in the sun. Soon, the woman began dragging some lightweight, wooden rocking chairs on the poach and then hung some signs on hooks above the porch rails, advertising Cordray's Mill grits and cornbread as well as Coca-Cola, Pepsi, and Budweiser beer.

Cleo finished dressing, walked down the sodden steps, and crunched through the still-damp gravel to meet the woman and get some fresh milk. It was only after she was halfway there, that she remembered Sam Lloyd's caution from the day before not to slip.

Joyce Cordray had told her that the store manager, Carolyn Sheffield, who was living in a duplex apartment in nearby Morgan, had been widowed when her husband was shot in a hunting accident. Joyce said that Carolyn was the perfect store manager. She knew everyone, and everyone liked her. She did not have any children of her own, so she spent time with every customer, talking to them and giving unsolicited advice while speaking with a direct kindness. Carolyn had been a single child, and the store was the only way she had a family in her life. She filled the role of being the mayor of Cordray's Mill.

As she walked onto the porch, she heard Carolyn from the interior through the screen door talking to the cat, who had rolled over on its back with its paws in the air, "Roscoe, you are about as sorry an excuse for a cat as there is in Calhoun County. I can see mouse droppings back here all over the floor. That's supposed to be your business. What do you have to say for your sorry self?" Cleo began to open the screen door as Carolyn continued her one-way conversation with the cat. "Don't make me come out there and –" Carolyn jumped when she saw Cleo at the door. "Oh, I didn't hear you come up. You must be the friend of Annie Mills that Joyce was expecting."

Inside the country store, Cleo found freshly made sandwiches and jars of pig's knuckles and boiled eggs, along with other local produce that awaited the hungry. Fresh-picked vegetables, and mayhaw, and blackberry jelly were available to carry home, along

34

with bags of cornmeal and grits from the mill. In a corner by the door, there was a cooler fortified with bags of ice along with the humming motor that kept the soft drinks, milk, and beer ready. Carolyn kept up a steady banter as Cleo familiarized herself with the store's offerings, and then she suggested they have coffee on the porch and get better acquainted.

When they were settled, a flight of wood ducks flew over, and Cleo was amazed to see them in formation. She looked around up and down the blacktop. "Other than the waterfall, there is hardly any noise here. You know, this is the first time in ... I can't remember, when I have been able just to sit and visit like we are doing. It seemed when I was living in the city, I was always running off to one thing or another."

Carolyn smiled over at her. "It is peaceful here. Most of us like it, but you may get tired of it after a while." As they sat, rocking on the front porch of the store with their coffee, Carolyn began to give her the history of Cordray's Mill. She was pointing to the mill. "Over there is one of the last stone ground grist mills in Georgia." She nodded across the street to the Cordray home. "When her husband got sick and could not work as he had before, Sam Lloyd, who had been his loyal worker for decades, stepped up to manage the mill. He dutifully reported every day's activity and progress and carefully handed over the cash from sales with a ledger of the transactions. After her husband died, Mrs. Cordray only had to think for a few minutes before naming Sam the new foreman and manager of the mill. It was

Sam who made that mill work as much as Mr. Cordray had." She sniffed a large breath. "Well, she soon heard from the county commissioners that she should have named a white man as manager, but she let them know right soon that her decision was made."

Carolyn stopped her story and rocked, thinking to herself, sitting on the porch that those jacklegs playing checkers down at the courthouse did not know anything about managing a mill, and Sam Lloyd had been Mr. Cordray's right-hand for more years than she knew. It was highly unusual for a black man in those days to be put in charge of anything, but Mrs. Cordray didn't care. She knew Sam, and knew he would do the job well, just like he had been doing for the past two years while her husband was sick.

Satisfied that her memory was correct, she continued. "She soon saw she had made the right decision because Sam came to work earlier and left later than ever before. He swelled with pride and showed what he could do. Mrs. Cordray told me that on the Sunday afternoon after she had named him the manager, several cars and trucks showed up at the mill, and a gaggle of black people got out all dressed in their Sunday go-to-church clothes. Bright white shirts and colorful dresses showed against the dark skin. Sam led them in and pointed out to them the workings inside of the mill, explaining how the wheel turned the stones and how he kept track of different customers' bags of corn, both raw and ground. After the crowd had *oohed* and *awed* for about twenty minutes, he led them back out,

36

locked up the mill, and tacked up a small plank on the side of the entrance door.

"Later that afternoon, after they had left, Mrs. Cordray told me she walked over to the mill. The late afternoon sun bounced off the water to reflect flashes of light in the shoreline trees, and it was in her eyes making it hard to negotiate the bridge. So, she had to use her cane to step carefully through the brush and gravel to the entrance. There she read, whittled into the wooded sign, "Cordray's Mill, Sam Lloyd, manager.""

When Cleo returned to her cottage from visiting Carolyn, she became nervous again about all that money in the suitcase half buried in the garage. She looked around but had no better idea where to put it. She couldn't go to a bank and did not know this area or anyone here she could trust who could help her. She had to find a more permanent place to hide it and quick. Then, on the outside chance, if the people from Boston found her down here, they wouldn't find the money. Without the money, maybe she could convince them she never had it. Those Boston crooks didn't know anyone down here they could pressure. That was an advantage for her. She thought she could count on Mrs. Cordray to stand up for her. She planned to fit in and make friends, so anyone coming from Boston would be a fish out of water. She looked back across the road and thought, if this was the backwater where she was destined to be for a while, at least when she left, she wouldn't go away poor. The people she had met here so far were nice, and she could do with some kindness in her life for a change.

Fishing

As John DuVall slowly motored through the stand of cypress trees, careful to avoid several protruding knees just out of the water, he noticed the waiting boat containing two fishermen. He recognized the men who came to this pond regularly from the nearby small town of Dawson. He slowed his boat to come alongside. "Afternoon boys. Having any luck?"

The older of the two shook his head like he'd been caught stealing a cookie from his mother. "You are a slippery fella. I'll give you that."

John put his motor into neutral and stretched by rolling his neck around. "Well, if you guys want to know where the big ones are hiding, you should hire me to take you rather than sneaking around, trying to find my secret places. That, or you could learn how to fish a little better so you can find them for yourself."

The man shook his head again. "John DuVall, you are a piece of work, and here you are giving us crap on top of it."

The other man said, "Nobody has been fishing around here as long as you have, so no one knows the places like you do. I hear you even squeeze way back up the creek dang near to Herod Dover Road."

John smiled. "Well, it pays to know the fish and where they come from."

The first man reached back to put the boat engine into neutral and then slowly wrapped the thick cord around and around in preparation to rope start the motor. He stopped and looked back at John. "Well, we all know you have your favorite places where you never take anyone else. We could hire you for a month, and you'd never take us there."

"You might be right, but you'd know for sure if you'd just hire me. I can promise you if you did hire me, you'd come home with some fish."

The man had finished wrapping the rope and was set to pull. "We'll think about it, but in the meantime, we'll be watching."

"You boys take care. Hope you catch your supper. Watch for water moccasins lounging in the trees." As he reached to put his motor back into gear, his foot kicked the tackle box, and the sound of metal clanking made him realize he still had his small .32 cal. pistol in the box. He kept it for snakes or other swamp dangers, and although he had never used it for any purpose, it gave him a sense of comfort. He moved on slowly as the man in the other boat pulled the cord to crank his motor.

Cleo and Carolyn

The next day, Cleo came back to the store. "Carolyn, sorry to bother you, but I don't have a phone number or a phone that works yet, and I thought maybe you could get a message," she hesitated, "to John, is it? My stove needs to be hooked up and checked out. I'm afraid I'm not good at that kind of stuff, and Mrs. Cordray said maybe this ... John, could help?"

"Yes. It's John DuVall, and he'll be glad to help. He may have fishing clients this morning, but I'll check. He's got two young boys that are seven and nine and come in here two or three times a day, and they can hunt him up. He'll be over to check on you either this afternoon or tomorrow morning for sure."

Cleo looked around. "Maybe I could get some of that cheese from the big round over there."

"Sure thing, honey. Just cut it yourself, and I'll weigh it over here. While you're at it, you might want to get some soda crackers or Vienna sausages. Folks around her like to have all that together as a snack or a full meal if you eat enough of them. I put some ice in the coke machine last night before I left. You can just reach in and pull one up through the groves from the lever if you want one."

Cleo gathered the items Carolyn had recommended and blinked as she read the ingredients on the Vienna sausage can. She murmured to herself, "Mmmm. Ends and pieces?"

She continued to read, murmuring to herself, "Mechanically separated chicken, water, salt, corn syrup. Contains 2% or less of beef, pork, dextrose, natural flavors, sodium nitrate, garlic powder." She made a face and put the can back.

Carolyn shifted her weight behind the counter. "Just bring that stuff and the cheese over here, hon."

Cleo looking around the store, commented, "Well, Mrs. Cordray's granddaughter was sure right about it being quiet around here."

"Maybe it's too quiet for you?"

"Sorry. I'm not sure what you mean?"

Carolyn looked out the door into the sunlight and then back at the attractive woman. "Just don't know what you are used to, I mean in terms of activity. It might be hard to believe it, but his place was much more lively years ago ... even a few years ago. Back then, everything around here was involved in farming, even more so than today. There were lots more people living in the country. Farming was not as mechanized back then, and it required more hands to do the work. All that began to drop off after World War II, and I think even that mess over in Korea slowed it down some. A lot of the crops are planted and processed in other places and with more modern ways ... combines and such." She nodded to her left. "The mill is sort of like a relic of older times. Now, only the locals still come here to use it."

She sighed as she stacked Cleo's purchases on the counter. Roscoe's head lifted from her sleeping position and smelled in the direction of the cheese with some interest. Both women ignored her as Carolyn continued, "The store income has also dropped off. I was looking just the other day and noticed that I'm ordering much less of all the inventory here than I did a few years ago. With the store, it's also mostly the locals who come to stock up. They're stuck in their ways and don't like to drive over to the larger towns much anyway." She looked out the door. "Even the gas sales are dropping. Traffic is down, and people just pass right on through. No one stops like they used to." She looked out the door and across the street at the house. "Joyce doesn't want to admit it, cause this area has been the main business of her husband's family for almost a hundred and fifty years, but maybe our best days around here have already passed."

Cleo, touched by the woman's lament, said, "That's too bad. Maybe you could do something to bring people back in here."

Carolyn frowned, "Like what?"

Cleo ducked her head slightly and smiled back at her. "Like have a dance over at that pavilion next to the swimming pool."

Carolyn stretched her back. "That would be something to see. Joyce Cordray told me in the heyday, the cars would be lined up and down the road out there on Saturday night with the people who came to dance when they had a real band to play for the crowds. They'd have lots of square dancing and had callers come in here from all over. They'd cover the wood floor in corn meal to let the dancers glide around smooth like for their feet which were tired from working all week." She shook her head and looked over in that direction. "That sure would be something to see again."

Ball Games

When Cleo walked from the store after visiting with Carolyn and crossed the road into the Cordray's yard, she saw two kids at play throwing a ball between them, who looked to be about the ages Carolyn had mentioned. She guessed they were Graham and Wallace, the sons of John, the local fishing guide and general handyman.

She stopped to watch them, using her hand to shade her eyes from the morning sun. "Hello, boys. What are two such charming and handsome young men doing out here?"

They froze.

She smiled at their discomfort. "You boys having fun?"

Slightly cautious, they looked at each other and then answered together, overlapping almost in one voice. "Yes ma'am."

While looking back and forth from one to the other, she walked slowly toward them. "Can I join you?"

Wallace, surprised, said, "What? You mean and throw the ball?"

"Sure. We had some real good ball players back where I come from ... champions."

Both boys were still looking at her in surprise, then at each other. Wallace shrugged.

"I learned a thing or two from watching and playing ball with my brothers." She rolled the top of the bag to seal it and put down her package. "Chunk it here."

Graham threw an underhanded slow ball with an arc to make it easy to catch.

She swung one arm backhanded to the side and snatched it from the air. "Come on, you can do better than that. She tossed an overhand ball straight to Wallace, who had to catch it with two hands and took a step back to secure it. He looked at Graham and smiled.

All three then backed up to give themselves space and began to throw the ball in a circuit to each other. Sometimes in a pitch, throw hard and direct, sometimes like a pop-fly. She stayed with them, then started throwing grounders, bouncing and skipping the ball through the grass to make them get low to scoop it up.

After about twenty minutes, they noticed John returning to the small dock off the side of Mrs. Cordray's yard. As the boat approached, Cleo nodded at it and told the boys she had to go home. They stopped playing to watch their father and his customers unload the morning's catch and fishing gear into their cars. The boys walked over to their father, who was securing the boat and cleaning up the spent bait and trash. "What you boys up to?"

Graham answered. We were just playing catch with that Miss Mansfield lady. "She can throw the ball real good."

Wallace then added, "She plays real fun."

John looked over at the guest house where the soft sounds of music from a radio were now drifting through the wire screen doors. "Well, one of you get the cricket box and the other the worm cans. You need to help me get me set up for those people coming here this afternoon from south of Albany."

Carolyn and John

John watched as his sons left to clean and refill the bait containers. Then, he finished securing the boat on the shore, tied it to a cement block with a chain, and entered the store to get some peppermint candy to give his sons for helping out.

Carolyn was anxious to talk to John, and as soon as he walked through the doorway, she began to tell him about the new resident in Cordray's Mill. "You just missed Cleo Mansfield. She pulled up the other night and asked to rent the empty house in the back over there." She leaned over the counter and looked through the screen door across the street. "She's got a big city air about her." She looked directly at John as he reached the counter, then nodded again across the street. She leaned in towards him conspiratorially. "Well, I don't mean to be too nosy. She's young but don't seem to be stuck up like city people can get. She's just sort of mysterious. Joyce told me she offered to pay cash in advance to rent the place. I'm guessing Mrs. Cordray would welcome that unexpected extra money. Mrs. Cordray said she noticed something of a sadness in her. You know, you'd think by all rights, pretty as she is, she should be sitting on top of the world." Carolyn leaned back and took a breath, pleased with herself at what she considered a thorough assessment of the new neighbor.

John nodded softly. "Okay. I'd like to get these four sticks of candy."

Carolyn reared back with her hands on her hips. "You don't seem too interested. That means you must not have seen our new neighbor yet. Huh? Like I said, she's staying at the guest house over there." This time she pointed across the street. "Said she knew Mrs. Cordray's granddaughter, Annie Mills, up there in Boston where she's from. Mrs. Cordray told me she had some real bad man trouble and needed to get away from him. I can see why. She is a looker! She's been in here to get some supplies, and we've sat and had coffee. Well, I'm not supposed to be talking about her so much but being as you will be seeing her come and go, I thought I'd give you a little background. She's gonna need some work done over at that cottage. You're not a bad-looking man yourself, John."

He shrugged as he pulled out some change for the candy. "How long she gonna be here?"

"Dunno." She made a phony laugh. "And here you are, acting like you are not in the least bit interested. Huh! Anyway, evidently, this man up there in Boston was harassing her, and she had to get away. I don't know the details. Joyce Cordray seems excited to have her here. I don't think her granddaughter or her daughter either one has that much to do with her anymore. They see us down here as a bunch of hicks. I guess this girl, well, young woman actually, must seem sort of like family to her even though I don't think they have ever met before. Still, it might spice things up to have some fresh blood around here."

John started to speak, but Carolyn was on a roll.

"I don't know what she did up there ... what kind of job and all. Mrs. Cordray's granddaughter is in some kind of fancy college, so maybe she's a teacher or something. Must be smart. Anyway, she put her car in the barn and covered it up. She told Mrs. Cordray something about being worried about the pecan trees dripping sap on it and messing up the paint. The granddaughter must have told her about that. Pecan trees sure will do a job on a coat of car paint."

John sniffed and looked across the street. "I thought that was from Aphids."

"Well ... whatever. It sure does mess up the paint job. Just look out there at my car! Those northern girls won't know what to do about it. Anyway, Mrs. Cordray asked me to take over some supplies and food and put them in the refrigerator and cupboard for the poor girl. The house still looks nice." She wrinkled her nose. "Smells real musty though from being closed up all this time. Needs an airing out. I took her some Air-Wick. Anyway, I'm thinking Mrs. Cordray might be needing you to check out the stove and stuff to make sure if it's all working like it should. Plus, you might need to make sure the roof don't leak."

John picked up the small sack of candy. "Okay, but I think I'll wait till they call me."

Carolyn reared back again with her hands on her hips. "Well … Cleo, that's her name, mentioned it to me. Her phone is not hooked up to call. They ARE asking for you. When you do manage to find the time to sashay over there, you just tell me if I's right about how that gal looks." She grinned and shook her head. "I'm guessing you might wish you would have gone on over there sooner. No offense, but those boys are going to be a handful to raise by yourself. Sometimes things just need a woman's touch. Like that time when your little Wallace stepped on that nail when you were way back up the creek fishing with those people from Columbus. You can thank your lucky stars that Joyce Cordray was around to get that hydrogen peroxide to clean it out before the lockjaw set in."

John didn't answer but picked up the bag of candy and nodded. He walked to the door with a look Carolyn thought was somewhere between embarrassment and guilt. When John left, she remembered the time with the wounded child. Everyone was upset. As she stood nearby holding the medicine and the bandages, no matter how hard Joyce Cordray tied to help the little boy, Wallace kept crying again and again, "I just want my mom."

That night John found the discipline not to have the several drinks he usually did after the boys were asleep. Instead, he looked at himself in the mirror without his shirt on and wondered what his future might hold. Though still young, he started to show his age, or maybe it was the miles. He decided to do a few pushups and sit-ups before bed.

Customer

Not long after John left the store, a truck skidded to a stop on the gravel outside. Getting out of the rusted pickup was an overweight woman with peroxide hair, distinguishing tattoos, and body piercings and carrying a pack of cigarettes in one hand. She tossed the empty beer can, that she was carrying in the other hand into a trash can as she entered the store. From across the street, Mrs. Cordray, watching from her porch chair, spoke to her dog, Gene Talmadge, as she often did, "There goes a complete Mississippi."

Seeing the woman enter, Carolyn put down the mail she was sorting to go onto the pigeonhole slots in the rack on the wall. Cordrays Mill was a designated postal drop, and she was the duly appointed postmistress. Usually, she just kept the mail in an alphabetical pile behind the counter and thumbed through the letters to find the correct envelope when one of the locals came by for food or gas. Pigeonholing was only done on the slow days.

As the woman rummaged through the store, Carolyn adjusted her reading glasses and reached into a cubbyhole on a wall rack, "Ruth Ann, here's your mail. It's been gathering up here for two weeks." She thumbed through it and laid it on the counter. "Based on these see-through window envelopes, it looks like some bills. It's not my business, but maybe you and Jerome might ought to think about that instead of more beer." Her cat, Roscoe, lying on the counter, sensed a disruption to his nap, jumped down, stretched, and walked to the back of the store away from the customer.

The rough-looking woman pounded a six-pack of beer on the counter, along with some cans of potted meat and a box of saltine crackers. She gave Carolyn a stern look. "We'll do what the fuck we want to do when we're good and goddamn ready." She nodded at the package of letters. "If you are so interested in our business, you can pay the fucking bills yourself." She slapped down a five, several ones, and some coins. "Here. Count it and give me my change and add a pack of Pall Malls." She looked out the screen door at the house across the street and sniffed strongly. "I see that old lady still got that … colored fella over at the mill. That's a job that should go to a white man. Get the money to them that really needs it … and deserves it." She sniffed again. "They already got that boycott and marching and shit going on up in Alabama. Stuck up bitch."

Carolyn packed the items into a paper bag and handed it to Ruth Ann, who had shifted her angry eyes from Mrs. Cordray's house across the street and back to her. "Have a blessed day, Ruth Ann."

Ruth Ann tucked the sack under the armpit of one shoulder and turned for the door, then stopped and looked back at Carolyn. "Another thing. That wheel of rat cheese back there where your cat hangs out sometime is getting a little crusty. Don't go an poison whatever customers you got left with bad cheese." She gave a satisfied toss of her head and banged out the screen door.

The Stove

Cleo opened the door to find a fit, handsome man who looked to be only a few years older than her, standing on the doorstep, holding a tool kit, who said, "Hi, I'm John DuVall. Carolyn said your stove needed a look and Mrs. Cordray also told me there was a struck window in the back room."

She smiled, appreciating his earnestness and straightforward way of speaking. "Yes." She stepped back. "Come on in. I'm Cleo Mansfield. Pleased to meet you." She put out her hand.

"Okay. Nice to meet you too." He sat down the tools and shook her hand, then leaned back into the yard and said in a raised voice, "You boys play out there. Don't break any of that shrubby. I'm gonna help this lady."

She looked past him to see the two boys she had played catch with the day before on the edge of the yard, throwing a baseball back and forth. As she stepped back further to allow him to pass, she noticed they were using similar patterns of fly balls and grounders as she had done with them when they had played together. Joyce's dog, Talmadge, was running back and forth between them, following the path of the ball.

As he began his work, she stayed with him, asking questions about what he was doing and about himself. He was hesitant at first, but she had learned how to draw a man out from working in the bar and soon had him laughing and telling her stories about himself. She gave him compliments and offered a Coca-Cola, which she had learned from Annie back in Boston that it was what Georgians called all soft drinks.

Although she had started the conversation just to get to know the man who seemed to be the only person near her age who lived within miles, she found that she enjoyed his openness and honesty. She liked that he was not worldly and did not try to act like he was something he was not. He was genuine, kind, handsome, and good with his hands. He was just under six feet and trim of build which made him only slightly taller than she was.

She noticed how he moved carefully and approached his work with thought and planning. When he moved to do something, he was self-assured with no wasted motion. He let his tools do the work and did not try to muscle the labor like some men did to show off. She could tell, however, that he was one of those wiry men whose muscles were compact and toned naturally more from work, the luck of genetics, and the challenges of life than by planned exercise.

Based on an idea she got from the Audrey Hepburn movie "Sabrina," she was wearing new tight pants and a checkerboard patterned shirt she had purchased on the way down to Georgia. She had tied the shirttail ends at the waist and had added a scarf around her neck in a soft knot to one side. It was the first time she had worn some of the new clothes she had gotten in Charlotte, and they seemed to be appreciated by the sidelong glances of John DuVall. As his work progressed, she could tell he was taking more time than he needed to finish. She used this opportunity to get him to talk more about himself and his boys playing out in the yard, and the conversation finally got more personal.

He put down the tool in his hand, looked out the window at the mill, and laughed. "You know, I used to work at that mill for fifty cents a day when I was a kid. I'd ride my bicycle all the way over from Morgan, where I lived with my parents." He leaned back against the counter, and then he became more pensive. "I was still sort of a kid when I signed up to go off to war, but I was not a kid when I returned. When I finally got out and got back down here to South Georgia, it was hard to find work, and my mother had caught cancer. Dad had run off during the war and nobody ever heard from him again. I did what I could to make a living and take care of her at the same time. Mrs. Cordray and Miss Carolyn helped, but we couldn't do much for her, and my mama died. After all, I'd seen overseas and seeing her dying just as I got back, well, it was a lot to take in.

"Anyway, I did not handle it very well and took to drinking more than I should. There was this gal that was a couple years behind me in high school, and she liked to party, so we got together, but it didn't turn out very good. Next thing … she got pregnant, and we got married." He tapped the counter with a knuckle and made a frown. "She didn't mean to be like she was, but I found out that her dad had

56

come onto her, and I think she saw me as a way to get out of the house." He sniffed and made another strained face.

"After the boys came, it was strange, not like it was supposed to be. She didn't pay them much attention. At first, she just cried a lot. Then she just wanted to get back to going out and drinking and dancing and such. We tried to work on it, and I tried real hard to make things last, but she just had this kind of need to look over the next hill. The boys needed her, and I needed her, but she wanted the high life. She liked to have men look at her. I believe she thought her true happiness was just down the road."

He turned to look out the window for a moment, took a breath, then turned back to her. "It was touch and go for a while, and I had trouble bringing in enough money for her and to take care of the boys. Again, Mrs. Cordray and Miss Carolyn pitched in to help. I don't know what I'd have done without them. Anyway, I came home one day from taking some people fishing, and she'd left. So, since then, it's just been me and the boys. When I'm off working at the fishing, doing construction, or whatever I can do for money, they kind of hang out over at the store or here at Mrs. Cordray's house. I mean, they go to school and stuff, but that's on the bus over to Morgan, and when they are back here, there is not much to do or not many people to see. Nobody else around their age."

Cleo's eyes dropped. "I kind of know what you are talking about with your wife. Men have been staring at me since I was in my early teens. You either like it and get used to it or not, but for most of us, it's never comfortable. It's kind of like having a sign on you. Sounds like she liked it too much."

"Yeah. Well, I–"

She interrupted him. "I lost a baby a few years back. I was not married or anything. Tried to work and be pregnant at the same time but had a miscarriage. I remember I was really depressed after that. Having a baby is a lot for a young woman to get used to. I'm not trying to take up for your wife or anything. It's just that I can understand that being pregnant does something to you, especially when you are struggling. I may know something of what she might have been feeling."

He looked down for a moment, thinking about what she said, then sniffed. "I'm not raising them right, much as I wish I could. Don't know how, but they are turning out to be good boys. Got smarts and don't seem to have a mean streak like some can. Wallace is more sensitive. He took his mother's leaving the hardest. He didn't have Graham's anger to protect him. I'm grateful there's good help here in Mrs. Cordray, Carolyn, and even Sam Lloyd. He likes the boys, and they play with his grandkids sometimes. It's kind of all I can do to keep food on the table, so they are helpful. Otherwise, I'd go off to find a better-paying job."

He picked up the wood plane he had left on the counter and put it in the toolbox. "Sorry, I don't mean to unload on you. I've never had anyone much I could really talk to about my situation. Don't let what I'm saying make you think I'm poor-mouthing or anything. I'm real happy to have the boys and to have a job here, and am grateful to Mrs. Cordray and everyone for the help."

Cleo thought here in front of her was this handsome local handyman who could fix a stove or do almost anything. He was more honest and open than many of the men she had known in Boston. Above all, he seemed to have the two traits she had felt were missing in most men she had met in the bar – duty and loyalty. She wondered if he was handy in other ways.

Out in the yard, as the boys played catch, they talked back and forth in a pattern each time they threw the ball. Joyce Cordray's dog, Talmadge, followed the ball and ran back and forth between them, hoping to catch the ball and be a part of the game.

"That lady is pretty."

"Not prettier than our mama, I bet."

"Don't know. I don't remember her much."

"Just look at that picture of her we got hanging in the hall."

"Think Daddy likes her?"

"Don't know. When he went inside the house, he was looking at her different from the way he looks at Mrs. Cordray and Carolyn."

"She's younger, is all."

"Maybe. Can't tell."

"Think she'll live here forever?"

"Too early to know. Just be nice to her."

"She seems nice. She's fun to play catch with anyway."

"Yeah. That's for sure.

Cleo and Sam

The next morning after coffee and another local history lesson from Mrs. Cordray, Cleo went to see the mill. As she walked across the bridge over the wooden dam that was connected to the earthen dam forming the south side of the lake, she listened to the sound of the water as the Ichawaynochaway Creek fell from the lakeside and dropped almost two stories into the fast-flowing stream below. She could see how the force of this power could turn the massive, wooden wheel on the side of the mill. Looking at it reminded her of the Ferris wheel at the fun park back in Boston.

The mill was located off the side of the road on a small red clay cliff of land that was part of the dam. That land rise between the road and the mill left just enough space for parking and transferring the grain. The building itself was made of sun-bleached, unfinished wood that rose in long, wide horizontal rows of boards toward the roof. As she reached the structure, she listened to the noise of grinding from the stones on the outside, but the sound of the falling water dominated most of what she could hear. She paused to knock loudly on the wooden door, then hesitated, thinking that it was unlikely anyone inside could hear her knock. Then, she pushed it open.

She had to pause and let her eyes adjust in the dim light to see past the dust in the one-room operation. The space looked smaller than she had expected. When she could see better, she was staring into the faces of two white men in khaki pants, standing to the side next to stacks of bags, some empty, some full. She assumed they were customers getting their corn ground. However, the way they were looking at her reminded her of some of the stares she had gotten back in the bar. Then, she realized the air everywhere was filled with power from the ground corn, further obstructing her view and stinging her eyes. She tried to wave it away from her face, and on the other side of the space could see Sam Lloyd and another man working the levers to make one massive circular stone slowly spin on top of another.

The two men staring at Cleo got Sam's attention, and he turned to see her backlit in the doorway. He pointed to his assistant to continue the grinding and hustled over to her, bowing slightly as he approached. "Oh, Miss Cleo, is it?" He smiled and shook his head. "This is not a good place for a nice lady like yourself." Then, realizing he might be sounding disrespectful, added, "Sorry, didn't mean you are not welcome, but I'm surprised to see you here, is all."

She nodded back and put out her hand to shake in greeting. "Yes. We did not get a chance to meet formerly when you came over to Mrs. Cordray's house the other day. Nice to meet you. I just wanted to see how the mill worked. Is that okay?"

He hesitated, looking at her outstretched hand, then shook it briefly, only touching the ends of her fingers. The two white men standing, waiting for the ground meal, looked at each other. One of them spat to the side.

Sam moved in hesitant steps and walked, bobbing in a bowing motion as he gestured at the stones and massive wood leavers. "You see ma'am, it's fairly simple. The corn is poured into a hole in the top, and this here series of levers and chains is attached to the water wheel outside. So, when it turns around, it moves the top stone. That stone grinds the corn against another larger stone on the bottom to crush it. Mr. Cordray fixed it so we could decide on how fine to grind the corn, to say grits or corn meal, by how close the stone wheels were placed in the grinding. The crushed corn comes out from a small chute on the side near the bottom of the contraption and into a sack."

He waved around in the air. "The rest of this just has to do leavers and stuff connected to the water wheel out there." He pointed through cracks in the wooden slats of the barnlike structure where the water wheel was slowly turning. "The water fills into the little trough-like things that are all around the circle, and it turns the wheel." He continued his explanation bowing up and down slightly as he spoke. "Yes'm, an we can make it hook up to turn these stones or leave it where it don't turn at all." Another bow with a sidelong glance at the two white men. He looked around like he was seeing magic. "When the wheel turns, there are teeth like nobs that catch other teeth inside here, and that makes the stones turn." He made a gesture with his hands and let the knuckles of his fingers slowly interlock.

He pointed to the central frame over the stones. "Yes ma'am. Mister Cordray, he set all this up like it is. He was a smart man. Now, Miss Cleo, I don't want to be … well, ma'am, this place is not good for a lady like yourself. It is full of all this corn dust, and it'll get all over you and something like to fly off the mill here and hurt you." Another slight bow.

She looked around once more. Nodded at the white men and said, "I understand. "Thank you for showing it to me." She guided herself back out the door and closed it behind her. Outside, she dusted the fine layer of crushed corn off her clothes and shook it out of her hair before recrossing the bridge and headed over to the store to visit Carolyn.

After her visit with Carolyn, she walked over to see Joyce Cordray and brought her the rent money they had agreed would be appropriate for the guest house. When she entered, Joyce looked up from the dining room table with papers spread all around. "Hello. You've caught me at my bookkeeping." She sighed and leaned back in her chair. "I used to do the books for my husband when he was alive, and I'm sorry to say, it does not take as long now." She looked at the papers. "It's mostly land rental for farming that brings in steady money these days. I've been trying to figure out a way to use the facilities here near at the bridge area to bring in more income. Maybe a restaurant or something?" She leaned back and shook her head.

"Let me know if you get any bright ideas."

Story Time

Graham and Wallace entered the store, one crowding just behind the other at their usual fast pace, and Graham was almost able to catch the screen door from banging shut. The look on Carolyn Sheffield's face reminded them of the discomfort she seemed to feel after she had given both of them several lectures on the subject of banging the screen door. She corrected them about almost everything they did, but she talked to them in such a motherly way they had learned to tolerate her and accept her direction.

About six months before, after Carolyn had kept them in an uncomfortably long discussion on correcting their unruly behavior, they had complained about her to their father. He quietly explained to them that she was just trying to help them. He said it was awkward for her since she did not have any children of her own. She was trying to do right by them, and they needed to respect her. He reminded them that she had known their mother and told them to think of her as a kind aunt who loved to see them and wanted what was best for them.

They did not tell their father that tolerating Carolyn was one of their favorite pastimes, bordering on a pleasure. They liked to play with her cat, who was supposed to keep the mice and rats away from the store merchandise, but who mostly slept. More importantly, Roscoe allowed the boys to rub over her and would purr when they massaged behind her ears. When she had had enough of the boys' attention, she would get up, stretch, jump down from the counter and disappear behind boxes of canned goods. When they asked Mrs. Sheffield about why she had a female cat with a boy's name, she shrugged and said the cat looked like a Roscoe.

The cat was, however, secondary to wanting to be with Mrs. Sheffield, corrections and all, because she entertained them for hours with her stories. Carolyn Sheffield was a widow with few hobbies. Her size prevented her from many activities other than working at the store and driving back and forth to Morgan, where she lived in a small duplex. For her recreation, she mainly went to the picture show. There were several small towns in the vicinity with a movie house, and some of them showed films even on weeknights.

During the times when activities in the store were limited, which was most of the time, she was available to tell the boys stories of what she had seen. Because she liked anything that was playing at the movies, there were a variety of stories to tell, and Carolyn was a good storyteller. She knew how to string a story together and highlight the exciting parts, including sound effects and gestures to illustrate her narrative.

As the boys entered, Carolyn gave an internal sigh at the wrinkled clothes with holes that needed patching. If John's wife had been any kind of a real mother to the boys, she would have been there to take care of things like that. That woman should have known better, whether she was still alive or was now watching them from above or, more likely, from below. She felt sorry for John, trying to raise two rambunctious boys and earn a living as a fishing guide and handyman in a place that was no more than a wide spot on a two-lane blacktop.

They came toward her, expectant and brimming with energy, each trying to get ahead of the other along the scuffed wood floor to the counter and the awaiting Roscoe. She looked over at the eggs and other produce safely in the cooler and the other chores she had completed around the store and figured everything else could wait. "How are you two boys today?"

Wallace spoke first, "We good Miss Carolyn."

Graham stopped stroking Roscoe, who was already flicking her tail back and forth in early exasperation at being disturbed from a mid-morning nap. He said in a louder voice than needed, "Did you go to the show last night?" That did it for Roscoe, who jumped down.

"Well hold your horses a minute. You boys ... stand here and watch the front for me. I gotta close up the ice door.

As she waddled to the back of the store, Wallace remembered a special time last week. When they came that day, Carolyn held up a large Maxwell House Coffee can heavy with water up to the brim and filled with some rocks below.

"Boys, my husband had these from when he was a young man 'bout the same age as you two. His grandma gave them to him, and I don't have a place for them anymore. I wonder if you two can take them off my hands and split them up between you without fighting."

"What is it?"

"Well, first, you gotta promise me about the fighting." They looked at each other and shrugged. "I'm gonna recommend you swap turns, each taking one piece and then the other one, and go back and forth. That sound all right to you."

Graham answered, "Yeah, I guess so, but we don't even know what it is."

"Okay, come with me." She walked out on the front porch and poured the contents of the full can onto the wooden boards of the porch. "There is the sunlight lay about fifty triangular pieces of flint rock." Carolyn continued, "These are mostly spear points, but around here, people call them arrowheads. You can see they are too big and heavy to fit on an arrow and then shoot it any distance. Although, there are some smaller ones that might work for that."

They were dumbstruck. Here was the greatest treasure any pre-teen boy could possibly imagine. Here was a pile of pristine and intact arrowheads. To them, it didn't matter what Carolyn had called the stones; they were plain, simple, and perfect arrowheads. They could see how the backs were notched to tie around the shaft and how the chips on the sides led to sharp edges and dangerous pointed tips. There were different shades of tan, brown and red colors in the rocks. One was all black. Already, each of them was picking which ones they wanted, and neither of the boys wanted to share. They wanted them all, or at least they wanted more than half. On the wood slats of the porch that morning, a trading war began between the brothers that lasted for their lifetimes.

Graham said quickly, "I dub firsts!"

Now, remembering that day the previous week when they had been given the arrowheads, Wallace looked over at his brother and smiled as Graham was thumbing through the few magazines on the counter. He was thinking of what he would trade Graham for one of the points he just had to have. As she returned to sit on the tall stool behind the counter, they noticed she was carrying a small paper sack.

She shook her head in a way that implied she had something to say that they would never accept. "Boys, you would not have believed it. I went to the show over in Arlington down there on the main street. They had this movie called 'From Here to Eternity'. There was everybody starring in it you ever heard about, including Burt Lancaster, Montgomery Clift, Deborah Kerr, Donna Reed." She stopped, took a breath, shook her head then leaned forward on the counter. "And ... you'll never guess who they had playing one of the soldiers," she leaned over further and looked back and forth between them, "it was Frank Sinatra." She leaned back to her normal posture. "He was GOOD, let me tell you. Not singing, but acting."

She stopped and looked around. "Oh, I almost forgot, I made these cookies and didn't want to eat them all myself, so I brought them to give the customers, but you boys can have one or two if you don't tell anyone.

Both hands reached out at once, and both said at the same time as they usually did. "We won't."

She leaned over towards them again, studying the boys being careful not to soil her new bright pink and green flowered print smock. "Graham, you need to button up your shirt all the way. It's not like a gentleman to leave it unbuttoned." She reached out and made the repairs to Graham's character, then turned to Wallace. "Let's see. You are almost all right, but you didn't get this smudge off your forehead." She licked a cloth and rubbed off the dirt. "There now, where was I?"

"Frank Sinatra was a soldier," said Graham.

"That's right, and they were all on an island called, Hawaii. We have big military bases over there smack in the middle of the Pacific Ocean. Do either of you know where that is?"

Both boys thought for a minute, then Graham said, "On the other side from the Atlantic."

"That's right. And that is off to the west from where we are now," she pointed out past the bridge and the Mill, "alllll the way across the United States and then halfwaaaay across the Pacific Ocean." Giving the directions winded her, and she took another deep breath. "So, let me tell you that Burt Lancaster is some good-looking man." She stopped and fanned herself in an exaggerated way like she always did when talking about good-looking men.

"You boys take a seat." They pulled a ladderback chair and a stool up near the counter and sat leaning forward with the cookies to listen.

"Before I start, I saw you throwing the ball the other day with Miss Cleo. Did you like that?"

Graham answered. "Yeah. She was fun."

Carolyn leaned back, hands on the counter, large and in charge. "So, maybe you ought to invite her to go fishing with you and your dad sometime. I bet she'd like that."

Wallace now piped up. "We will. Good idea. Now how about the war movie?"

Carolyn tapped the counter twice. "Well, all these men were training for war." She held up an imaginary machine gun and shifted her bulk right and left while saying in her gun voice, "Baaaaaa." At this unusually loud noise, Roscoe scatted from behind the crates of canned pears and peaches, and out the back door through the hinged flap.

Later, she heard the boys out playing cowboys and Indians and noticed that they included sound effects noise outside of the threatening dialogue. She smiled when they tried to imitate her creaking doors, gunshots, and menacing footsteps she had first heard on the radio and at the movies.

Back in Boston

When the remaining Brinks depository robbers learned that Rhonda had died bleeding from hemophilia after her injuries, their total focus became on finding the money. After a very thorough search of the apartment building had revealed nothing, one of them remembered the roommate, Cleo, something or another. Some snooping and talking to the neighbors revealed that Cleo had skipped town. She must have taken the money. Good, now at least they had a likely target and a way to get their money back.

Leaning on the other people at the bar where she had worked turned up several clues. Cleo had dropped the man-trouble story on one of her associates at the bar when she left to help cover her tracks for leaving. To the Brinks robbers, that fiction reinforced their idea that Cleo had stolen the cash. They began to sift through the background of anyone who might lead them to Cleo. After a process of elimination, one of them, that friend of hers, the naive college girl, seemed to be the most promising. They realized that with her, they needed to be more subtle. You couldn't just go and threaten a student at one of those fancy Boston colleges, so they came up with a plan that involved one of the waitresses at the club. With one of the robbers standing over her, she called the student, Annie Mills, claiming to be one of Cleo's best friends from the bar.

She said that Cleo had not picked up her back pay and that several letters from her family had arrived addressed to her at the bar that looked important. As the man watched and listened, in a whisper, the woman from the bar told Annie that she sure didn't want to do anything to get Cleo in trouble. She said that Cleo's good friends, like Annie, had to defend her from that nasty man that had been bothering her. She wanted to protect Cleo by sending the letters and the money to a place where she could collect them on the sly. Could she help? Maybe she knew a post office or general delivery or even someone else's mailbox near to where she might be staying? To be on the safe side, Annie should not tell anyone that Cleo was going to be getting a package. Yes, of course, she would put a note in the package to tell Cleo that Annie had said hello. Annie was, sure enough, a good friend. Cleo would be so grateful.

The remaining Brinks robbers were surprised that it was so easy to get the information they needed from the college girl. Next thing they got to a map, and … where the hell was Cordray's Mill, Georgia?

Albany

Cleo put on a nice dress for the trip. She offered to help Joyce Cordray by taking some bags of corn meal over to the Colonial Grocery Store, which sold them at their location on Slappy Drive in Albany. She also needed some things that were not available at Carolyn's store, or in the nearby village of Morgan. She had heard that there were a couple of good pharmacies in the larger town, and she wanted to give the department and clothing stores over there a good look. She needed a break from the country and figured that a larger town must have things going on that would be more interesting for her to do.

As she entered the barn to get her car, she glanced over at the pile of sacks and tarp under which she had hidden the suitcase. It made her cringe to realize yet again just how bad a hiding place that was. She'd have to find a better place and soon. Then she saw the Massachusetts tag on her car crying out for attention. Another thing to do. She had been debating about getting a Georgia tag but was unsure how much paperwork that would require or if they would dig into her past to transfer the car's tag here in Georgia. Nothing was simple, and all of it made her nervous.

Still, she was not going to stick her head in the sand. She was not going to be some mealy mouth wall flower and lose herself even in this strange and dangerous situation. There had to be a happy medium.

She looked over again at the pile of rags covering the suitcase with the money that would finance her future. On an impulse, she grabbed another handful of money from the suitcase and reburied it using the trash from the floor. Then nervously, she tossed several more paper sacks on the top of the stack. That would have to do until she could find another solution. When she turned the key, the car started. Thank God the battery had not died on her.

After her shopping, Cleo saw that Albany had a Carnegie library, and there she was able to look up information on the Brinks robbery. She found that the money that had been stolen from the Brinks depository was a pile of old bills that were slowly being taken out of the allotment to make way for changes in a new design. The treasury department planned to slowly release the newly printed bills to cover those being removed from circulation over several years' time. What she had in the suitcase did not belong to anyone or any bank. The money she had was not intended to be used to finance a car or a house. It did not come from anyone's savings. It was just extra money-based on an older design that did not belong to anyone or any bank. It was still as good as anything out there, and no one would miss it. She was home free.

She read that in addition to the cash, there were coins and other securities stolen. She figured that before they put it in the suitcase, the thieves must have traded off the coins for paper money and cashed out the money orders and securities or other valuables also to get cash. This made her realize that what she had in her possession was untraceable, and its loss would not be personally felt by anyone. She leaned back and, for the first time, felt some relief from her situation. Then she realized that the thieves were after the suitcase for the same reason.

As she was walking past the front desk of the library to leave, newspaper headlines caught her eye about an ongoing bus boycott in Alabama and black people there marching for civil rights. She stopped to glance through the paper and read that the marchers who were breaking the law were being led by what the newspaper referred to as some outside agitators from the north. After leaving the library, she walked across the street to the New Albany Hotel to get lunch in their dining room. Sitting in a nice hotel dining room with flowers in a small vase resting on the center of the tablecloth, she felt herself relax. It was almost like she was back in a city again. She decided to take her time. The meal and especially the chocolate pie for dessert was delicious.

Magic Stick

Sam Lloyd was loading his truck to return home after a long day when he noticed John DuVall's boys. As the only kids living there, the boys were all over the place, playing games or fishing almost every day they weren't in school. Usually, the boys' high energy and enthusiasm, as well as their noise level, continued until bedtime with a volume that gave anyone in area, a good idea of their location. Now, Sam observed they were reaching an age where they noticed things more closely and began to be more circumspect in their activities.

The house where they lived with their father was behind the store on a dirt road through a patch of woods on the other side of a ravine. At the bottom of the ravine, a creek formed by the runoff from nearby fields wandered and eventually fed into the stream below the dam and the mill.

Over time, the boys had cut a narrow trail through the woods on either side of the ravine leading to the store, mill, and Mrs. Cordray's wide front lawn. That was the area where they played and occasionally met other kids near the main road. Their father had installed an old iron school bell by the back porch of their small house, which he would ring when he wanted them to return, and the *gong* sound that carried throughout the woods let them know it was time to head home.

They had begun to dread the time when the shadows of the dark called on them to trek back through the woods and the ravine to their home. In the evening, as the gloom of night was settling into the ravine, the boys would stop after a day of play that included imagining monsters, gorillas, outlaws, escaped convicts, and various other creatures. This was the time when melancholy encroached to turn their daytime fantasies into wholly possible and probably lurking realities. On those occasions, when they heard the unexpected gong summons, Wallace and Graham would steel themselves for the task ahead to avoid the demons and then run full tilt down one hill through the ravine and up the other hill and toward the light and safety of their home. Sometimes, they would trip over roots and fall or scrape themselves on the branches of trees hidden by the night. To the boys, these bumps, bruises, and cuts were, however, much preferable to the forest terrors that would surely have grabbed them had they dawdled.

On this evening, as Sam Lloyd watched the boys, he could see the worry on their young faces as they stood on the ridgeline of the hill behind the store. They were rocking back and forth, summoning the courage to aim for the runaway path, still visible from the store's back porch light shining into the dark. From the opposite hilltop, the safety from their home's dim glow beckoned on the other side of the ravine.

Curious, Sam came over and asked what they were doing. Embarrassed, they tried to make excuses for their fears but fell short of being manly in their explanation. Standing on the edge and casting glances into the small dark valley, their answers continued to ramble evasively. Seeing their fears, Sam stopped his approach next to them and put his hands on his hips.

"Okay, now I understand," he said, looking around at the ground. "What you say makes a lot of sense." He stepped to his left. "You know," he said, then he thought for a minute, still looking around, "I'm going to do something for you. Ah, there it is." He bent down and picked up a two-foot-long stick that was lying on the ground. "Here it is. I thought I might have lost it, but here it is, right where I left it. This, here, is my magic stick." He gave it a wave.

By this time, he had their full attention.

"Now when you got to go through the woods at night, you jus take this stick and hold it like this." He tightened and then loosened his grip on the stick. "Jus like this," shaking it slightly. "Now you try it. Mmmmm huh, that's it." He made a slight correction. "Now, let your brother try it." They each grabbed the magic stick and held it like Sam had done, moving it, showing that they knew how to use it while also seeking his approval.

"That's right. You got it. Now when you go down the path over there in the dark toward home, you don't need to run no more. If you come on something that looks like a bear or a ghost or something, just hit it with this stick, not too hard, just kinda touch it, and immediately it will turn into a bush."

81

They both rocked back on their heels.

"Now, don't you worry. Even if you lose this stick, once you use the magic stick, you got the magic with you, and any old stick will do.

Cleo and John

It turned out that there was more than one stuck window in Cleo's rented home. John was called again, and he came with his hand plane and sandpaper. She said apologetically, "I hope I'm not being too much of a bother getting this place back in shape." She was wearing the tight pants he had noticed before and a ruffled, off-the-shoulder senorita blouse.

John tilted his baseball hat back on his head. "You are no bother at all." He looked around the room and then back to her. "For the better part of several years, this house has been empty, and it's normal for things to get out of whack." He nodded at the window. "This stuff needed doing anyway. Besides," he gave her a polite smile, "it's nice to have a lady with some class around here." Now the smile broadened warmly. "Mrs. Cordray did a good day's work when she invited you here. You dress up the place."

Cleo laughed. "I think Mrs. Cordray has put me a notch or two up the social ladder from where I belong. I did meet her granddaughter. That's how I know about this place. But ... ah, I met her in a bar where I was working, not in a fancy classroom or a tea party. I did get to know Annie Mills - I think Cordray is her middle name, and she is a very nice girl. Let me add in my defense, pouring liquor in a bar wasn't the only job I could get, but it was by far the best paying job I could get, and I needed the money." She took a deep breath, and her face clouded. She remembered having to send money to her family for over a year to hire a lawyer when one of her brothers had gotten into trouble.

She sat on a stool by the counter. "It was later when I got into this situation where I had to leave town and go far away, that this place Annie had told me about came to mind. So, I called her, and she called her grandmother, and here I am. I think her granddaughter gave Mrs. Cordray a sort of embellished description of me, but I'm glad she did." She looked around. "I'm probably the first person from Boston that has ever been here." She smiled. "It's a pleasure to know there are some people like you around here, you know, more my age to talk to."

He sat down the wood plane and dusted his hands. "I think I'm the only one around here near your age, well, not married or something."

Cleo quickly continued. "I appreciate you helping me with the windows and the stove and, all of it." She hesitated. "Your boys are adorable."

He looked out the window and then back to her. "Well, be careful. They'll latch on to you and be underfoot. There're not many people around her to talk to or play with. When I'm working, and they aren't in school, they hang out and can get into anything they find that interests them." He gave her a nod. "I'm guessing they'll

84

find you very interesting." He smiled and turned to finish sanding the window seal.

She looked out the window into the yard at the boys running around, shouting and laughing. "That's not the worst fate anyone could have. I'd like to invite all of you over for supper tomorrow. Would that be all right?"

Finishing, he blew the wood dust out through the screen, shut the window, opened it again, then shut it and nodded. "Be ready for rowdy." He put his tools in his portable toolbox and picked it up.

She laughed. "I had brothers. Besides, by then, I'm likely to have found something else that I need you to fix." This comment caught him in his step toward the door. He hesitated and thought she seemed to be looking for more subjects to discuss as she continued, "I just love to see the lightning bugs here at night. I don't see them where I come from. And the moss in the trees, it's all just so romantic and lush."

He shook his head from side to side. "Don't pick up the moss; it's got redbugs in it. They're Itchy. The lightning bugs are pretty. The boys catch them and put them in glass jars with holes poked in the tin lid to give them air. They carry them around like a flashlight at night sometimes, but usually, they are all dead by morning." That comment seemed to bother her, so he hastened now, finding a way for him to prolong their discussion. "I don't mean to be speaking out of line, but Carolyn over at the store told me a little more about your

… situation … I mean more than you told me the other day." He hung his head for a moment, slightly embarrassed, then looked at her. "You don't need a radio to keep up with the news around here. Anyway, she … it happened. Sounds like you don't have any immediate cause to go back to Boston, so maybe you just need to make the best of it down here."

She smiled at him and put a hand on his arm. "What you say sounds right to me."

A flush went through him from her touch. He swallowed. "We don't know each other very well, and although, like you said, we are the only two people around here the same age and … I guess, I meant if you ever wanted to talk to somebody."

There was a loud noise and whoops outside. He opened the screen door and shouted outside. "Boys don't be running into that shrubbery of Mrs. Cordray. Stop swatting it with that stick. If you knock the buds off her azaleas, she'll have your hides." He turned back to her. "Thank you. It's been good to get to know you. I'll … see you soon. I mean tomorrow night."

"If not before."

"Yeah."

"Good. You and your buddy Sam Lloyd seem to be the only men who can do things around here. Glad to have you two around."

John hesitated. "Well, we are not exactly buddies. We kind of work together sometimes, but it was not always like that. When I first come around here, I was younger and had a kind of an attitude. I may have said some things in passing to him that were not as nice as they could be. After I got back from the war, I was smarter, I guess, and we've been good together since then. I sure do respect him. We've just never hung out together. Difference in age and all."

She digested what he said and what was unsaid. "Okay." She looked out the window at the mill and took in a deep breath, then looked back at him. "Well, then, maybe I can get you to take me fishing sometime. I've just heard about it, but I've never been … fishing, I mean. The boys mentioned it."

He gave her a serious look, and then he smiled. "Love to, but be forewarned, the bait is kind of nasty." He nodded and headed into the yard to round up his sons.

On a Walk

Cleo was coming back from a late afternoon walk when she saw Sam securing the mill for the night. He noticed her and hesitated as she approached his truck and began to speak, "Thank you for explaining to me how the mill worked the other day. It was interesting and so simple in a way. I just had never seen how things like that worked." She shrugged.

He finished putting some cornmeal bags into his truck. "Yes ma'am. I hope you didn't get your clothes all dirty. It's not an easy place to be when the dust's flying around like that."

She smiled. "I'm not that fragile. Sometimes you men think women can't handle anything physical or unpleasant. We've been doing it all our lives while you guys got to go off to work or sit around and be lazy."

He nodded politely at her and then over to the mill. "Yes'm. It's just you coming to visit the mill is unusual around here, is all. I spec you are the first lady other than Mrs. Cordray to even be inside there when the wheels were turning and dust flying."

"Well, you didn't seem to mind, but I had the feeling those two men who were your customers were more upset. Could it have been because when I was there visiting, I was talking to you and not to them?"

Sam stopped still and appeared to think about her comment for a moment. "Ma'am." His shoulders dropped a little. "I don't know about that, but it was just unusual all the way around. Nothing on you. Just unexpected. You're welcome and all, just folks down here may not be used to seeing things and doing things like they might be used to up in Boston."

She nodded in acknowledgment. "Well, let me ask you something. You've been around here for a long time, and maybe in years past, you saw how it used to be at the pavilion with dancing on the weekends and such."

They both paused their conversation at the noise of a pick-up truck crossing the bridge, passing them, and then rambling on towards Morgan. After the truck cleared, Sam looked across the bridge at the empty building and smiled. "There is a jukebox over in there now. It used to be a heap more lively. Even after the war, there were bands playing here almost every weekend." He scuffed the dirt with his toe as he remembered. "My wife and I would sometimes come and park over here by the mill just to sit and listen to the music from across the creek. A fella who goes to my church had a band, and they would come here to play for ... the people. Back then, it was still the smooth jazzy big band music that filtered across the road over here. They also liked to square dance in those days, and my friend had someone in his group who could also play that lively music with the fiddle. Nowadays, with that jukebox blaring, it's more like hearing loud electric guitars and teenagers screaming. The pace of the world has become a lots more noisier."

She said, almost absentmindedly, "Maybe we can switch it back around." She turned toward her home. "Okay. Well, I think I interrupted you as you were headed home, and I don't want to make you late."

"Yes, ma'am. Thank you. You take care of yourself." He got in the truck as she moved back onto the edge of the highway and continued her slow walk back to her house, head down, thinking.

Joyce Cordray and the KKK

Joyce Cordray recognized the pickup truck bumping up her driveway with a sign on the door advertising auto repair. It contained three young men she knew to be members of the local Ku Klux Klan. She walked onto the porch to meet them as they piled out of the truck and ambled up towards her steps. Talmadge, sensing unknown intruders, moved to stand behind her watching the strangers.

As they approached her, the driver nodded. "Morning, Mrs. Cordray."

She stopped at the top of the steps, standing with her cane leaning to one side as a barrier to them coming onto the porch. "Jessie, what trouble you and these boys looking to get into today?"

He quickly answered. "No trouble, ma'am. No trouble at all. We just checking on something we heard about a Yankee gal moved in near here." He looked left and right as if he expected to see a soldier clad in a full-blue uniform lurking behind a tree. "We just want to make sure everyone around here is protected from the wrong sort."

Joyce rolled her eyes and pushed out the breath she had been holding, which made her cough. "Well Jessie, I appreciate your interest in my well-being. But just so you know, and try to remember this in the future, even if you need to write it down. I'll rent to whoever I want to and don't need to ask you or tell you about it."

He pushed his hands in a jerking motion toward her as he took a step back from the porch. "No. Don't get me wrong. We jus didn't want you to get tied up with the wrong kind of person. They already got them Yankee agitators up in Alabama. We don't need 'em here." He looked over his shoulder across the street. "You already got the wrong kind of person over there at the mill. Segregation means those kinds of people," another jerk of his shoulder toward the mill, "shouldn't be having the jobs white people should have."

She crossed her arms over her chest and leaned back slightly. "Just hold into your horses, young man. I've got the person running my mill that I want to. We may not be living by it here just yet, but I understand they passed some new laws to change how we are supposed to do things. That man, Sam Lloyd, learned everything my husband was here to teach. He's the same person who was working alongside my husband, keeping that mill repaired and running it when you were still in diapers. I didn't see you around here asking how it was done. No sir. That job is for the man who knows how to do it, not some freebie to a freeloader." At this comment, the other two men laughed. Jessie gave them a quick look which shut them up.

She continued. "I'm still friendly enough with the sheriff, to let him know I don't need you coming over here and bothering me. I'm sure you don't need him visiting you and learning any more about whatever it is you do when you go sneaking around at night. Now you boys go on back to your shop or wherever you hang out, and let me live my life in peace. I'm old enough to be your grandmother and don't need your advice … about anything." Talmadge, sensing the tenor of the conversation and the raised voices, moved to the edge of the porch and watched the men in the yard closer.

Jessie shrugged, put his hands in his hip pockets, and leaned forward slightly. "Well, ma'am, we just kind of want to make sure our town and the community round here is safe from the wrong kind of people and outsiders, like they got up in Montgomery." Jessie shrugged northward, then turned to give the yard and the mill another hard look. He ended his search back on the porch with Mrs. Cordray. "Anytime we can help keep things steady, you can call on us." He then nodded to his friends, and they got back in the truck and left.

Fishing

Mrs. Cordray had continued the tradition her husband started of having a compost pile in the rear of the backyard. The jumbled stack of debris included leftover food, leaves, dirt, bits of newspaper, and a significant pile of cow dung from a nearby farm which composted to produce a sometimes-smoldering pile of well-perfumed earth that was the abode to thousands of red wiggler worms, who called the mass, home.

Turning over a pitchfork of the compost pile produced enough worms for most fishing expeditions for John DuVall. Joyce Cordray knew how much he needed the money, so she let him use the pile to grow his bait which allowed him to charge a little more to his fishing customers. She even left a few of the empty Maxwell House coffee cans out there in case he did not have any containers handy for the worms.

Today, she watched as an unusually happy group walked across her front lawn to leave for fishing. Cleo was kidding the boys who stayed close to her side. John was trailing them, carrying the fishing tackle, and seemed totally smitten with her. John's diversion to the new neighborhood attraction had become a pattern in the past few weeks, and she had begun to wonder if she were to call John to do something for her if he would have to check with Cleo's schedule first. She and Cleo had not had coffee or sat together to talk in over a week now. The budding romance was not entirely unexpected, but it did present a new dynamic to the small community, and she was concerned that if there were problems between John and Cleo, it could move in a disappointing direction that might affect everyone else.

She looked out at the cottage behind her home and thought of all the years she had kept it empty and ready for one of her other relatives to use as a guest house, or for their permanent home if they ever returned to live here. Trying to handle the land rentals, the sharecropping, the mill, the store, and everything else her husband's family had owned was becoming too much of a chore. Someone needed to take over for her. She could see the decline and the change, and she was tired of struggling alone.

People just did not come here much anymore, and the mill was hardly breaking even. Her finances were being stretched, and before Cleo had arrived, she had begun to think of renting out the cottage to strangers. That created its own set of problems, because she worried about who might move in so close to her and then turn out to be a bad tenant. She felt she was losing the power to influence everyone and everything around here. That was an authority that she and her husband's family used to be able to command without it being questioned.

Before this new attachment between John and Cleo, she had begun to think that maybe this young woman could help her collect the rent from the leased land and maybe help with other things as well. Now, she was unsure.

The flat-bottomed boat rested on the shore, anchored by a cement block on the bank tied to a thin chain. There was a small dock that provided access to the boat. He entered first, bringing the anchor with him, and took his place in the rear by the motor as the boys clamored in, used to sitting side by side in the center. He steadied the johnboat in the water, holding onto the dock for her and then used the paddle to push them off from the shore. She wisely left the boys to their usual domain in the boat's center and sat carefully on the front seat, the furthest from John. She was aware of her size and the weight distribution the boat needed to maintain stability. This perch did allow her to look back at John and admire the family picture of him and his boys, all of them very mindful of her presence.

As the boat cruised slowly into the open water, he nervously told her the lake's history and some of the adventures he and the boys had had while fishing. Her presence changed the atmosphere of the family fishing trip and made it more formal, and she could feel his need to please her. When John's tour guide narrative mentioned alligators, snakes, and the storms that came up unexpectedly, the boys joined in with urgent, loud comments, each trying to outdo the other. Their stories always illustrated how brave they were in the face of any unexpected danger.

She replied with comments that respected the bond they had as a family and supported the protective way John included the boys in the conversation. She complimented the boys on their ability with the bamboo poles, baiting the hooks, and how they watched carefully for a bobble from the corks. She was dutifully compliant when they shushed her as fishing was supposed to be a quiet activity lest the fish hear their conversation and get spooked.

Even so, as the day continued, they could hear the fish they caught under them sloshing in the water container that made the base of the hinged bench used as the center seat. As the day advanced, most of the conversations were between her and the boys. John never added much to what was said, but just watched her from under his soiled, long-brimmed hat, like the ones she remembered baseball players wore.

It was a clear, beautiful day on the water where egrets and herons dotted the shoreline, and occasionally, wood ducks flew past in the clear sky reflected on the still lake. The moss hung thickly from cypress trees, and the dull gray made the blue-green of their overlapping needles look like braided hair. Later they ate the sandwiches she had made, and she turned her head respectfully when the boys stood to pee off the edge of the boat.

They moved over to one side of the lake under the shadow of a fallen tree. There was a large branch covering the angle of the tree, and as she ducked down, the boys reached up to move it aside so that when they all bent over together, the boat, could move through. On the other side, the water opened wider into a hidden lagoon. She noticed that the boys seemed surprised at coming to this new location. They looked back and forth from their father to this new lady accompanying them. It was clear to her that where they were headed was a secret place that, before now, had been just for them.

John quietly explained to her that this area was his favorite fishing hole. It was almost a separate pond surrounded by thick vegetation. Near the back side was an enormous cypress tree almost 12 feet in diameter that had been missed by the loggers 200 years earlier. It was surrounded by a profusion of knees protruding out of the water near the massively thick base.

He dropped anchor, and the boys, with the expectation of biting fish, put on a fresh worm and dipped their hooks into the deep-water hole in front of the tree. He relaxed now, leaned against the motor, smiled, and looked at her more directly and with clear interest.

She watched the boys trying to contain their excitement of being at the center of the world of fishing. They took to their task and were competitive, whispering to each other over who caught the larger fish while reaching for another worm. She gave them both compliments as each fish was pulled into the boat, and John helped to unhook them and drop them into the center seat container while the boys stood for the transaction. Several times she looked up from smiling at the boys to him, and every time he was watching her. Later that afternoon, when they returned to the shore as the sun touched the trees, and he took the fish to clean, she asked them to return to her home, where she had promised to cook the fish for supper.

The Flat Tire

Sam Lloyd had to go home for lunch to see about one of his grandchildren who was sick. On his return to the mill, he spotted a car on the side of the road with a flat tire. When he got closer, he saw that it was Miss Mansfield trying unsuccessfully to change the tire, and she looked exasperated and helpless on the seldom-traveled two-lane road. He pulled his old pickup truck to the side behind her.

"Miss Cleo, you done got yourself in a mess out here. Let me see if I can help."

Her expression changed from concern to relief when she saw it was Sam. "I'd sure appreciate it. I'm not much good with these mechanical things. I think I've got the wrong size wrench in this car to get this tire off. Glad you came along. I haven't seen any cars since I had the flat."

He smiled as he walked to a toolbox in the back of his truck. "Not likely to, either. This road is not much used, and it's chock full of holes." He pulled a four-prong cross universal lug wrench from his truck and got to work with the jack. "If you don't mind my asking, how come you are out here on this road in the first place?"

"Well, I've been over to Edison. I wanted to see that factory where they make those children's clothes. I was going to look to get something for John's boys. Unfortunately, they only make clothes for babies. I thought that this road might be a shortcut back to the house, but I must have picked up a nail."

He continued, carefully placing each lug nut on the inside of the hub cap, lying open like a soup bowl by the flat tire. "Well, ma'am, it's a good thing I came along. You could have been here a while, and it might not be a good idea for you to be out here all by yourself."

"I sure appreciate the help." she paused. "Carolyn over at the store told me you had a son that was in Korea and got hurt."

He stopped and bowed his head before answering. "Yes ma'am. He wanted to get out of here to live someplace else. We tried, but couldn't get him to stay home. My son's prideful and asked to enlist in the army. They trained him, and he was with the 24th Infantry Regiment. They were all colored troops. Well ... they had a company commander who was white. I don't mean to be talking disrespectfully of anyone, but everyone said that he was not good enough at his job in the white units and was reassigned after making several bad mistakes to go to the colored outfit. My son said he made several more mistakes, made bad decisions, and the unit morale was very low. Anyway, my son got wounded and came home later in 1952."

"I'm really sorry. How is he doing?"

"Cause of being hurt, he, he's not been able to find much steady work, so he's living at home with me and my wife. The friends he grew up with and went to school with around here, well, they don't have much to do with him. So, we make do." He took off the flat and wrestled the spare onto the hub.

She shook her head. "My brother was killed over there. It kind of changed everything for our family. Me, for sure. I had to go to work doing....." She took in a deep breath and changed the direction of the conversation. "How is your wife? I don't think I've ever even seen her."

Sam hesitated. "Well, Miss Cleo, she stays over in Shellman most of the time. She's helping to look after our son and his wife and kids. She works cleaning houses around there."

Cleo blinked, understanding that this meant cleaning up after white people. "Sam, I'm not from here and ... well, you can just call me Cleo if you like. I'm not used to all this formality."

He did not reply but screwed on the nuts loosely and picked up the four-way tire iron, fitted the head over one of the lugs, and gave it a spin. "Yes'm. I appreciate what you are saying, but maybe we need to," ... he fitted the wrench on another nut and spun it ... "kind of keep things like folks here are used to." He gave it a tightening tug. "You seem like a lady who speaks her mind. So, I'll answer you like it was just between us two." He thought for a moment. "All us folks

102

around the mill are kind of like a family of sorts, but other folks who come there might not understand that."

He moved to finish the other lug nuts. "You see Miss Cleo, my grandmother was born a slave. Now, I'm the manager of the Cordray's Mill. The manager." He stopped and looked at her. "I don't know of no other man like me that has a job with any kind of a title or that kind of responsibility. Folks where I live, and in my church, look at me, and they see success. I need to protect that. People round here need to see a successful black man.

"When white people, like white people from Boston, say something or make other people mad, after a while, most of them just let it drop and go on to do whatever they want to and forget about it. If I was to do something that made people mad, I'd not only not have my title and responsibility taken away, but I'd also not have a job. I need that job to feed my family. You can't eat self-respect."

She took a step toward him. "But people seem to like you. I don't see any racial animosity toward you."

"That's just it. I work to keep it like that. When you are looking at someone in the eye, and it's just you two, well, most people, unless they have a reason not to, can be right civil. One on one or in working situations and all ... everyone is more equal."

He adjusted his knees where he had been squatting. "It's when people get in larger groups when they don't feel like they need to be so polite that the mean stuff comes out. Some folks that might want to seem like they are bad, don't need much of a reason to act on it in a group. Sometimes people do mean things when they need to show off to others. Miss Cleo, I know what I'm doing. I know how it might look to people like you. I act like I act, and it is not a big price to pay for me to have a good job and some pride in myself, you know, inside. Someday things will get better. I still want to be here to see it."

She wiped her hands on her dress. "I'm just uncomfortable with all the way people want to control other people just because of the color of their skin, but I don't want to cause you or anyone any trouble. I just think you are letting all these people walk all over you. You don't have to do that."

He gave her a nod. "I understand what you trying to say, and I appreciate that sentiment. But … you got to try to see that pretty much none of the white people around these parts think a black man should have my job. They always after Miss Cordray to get some white man to be the manager. She might not admit it, but it cost her business to have me there. I owe it to her and to myself, and to all the other black folks around here to prove I deserve it.

"I'm trying to keep that job by working hard, being honest, and treating everyone else with respect. So, if by treating all those folks with lots of manners, maybe even more than they deserve, means I can keep the job, I'm gonna do that.

"Folks over where I come from look at me and think maybe I'm just the first one, and one day maybe they can get to a place where they can have more respect. So, I got to do what I think is right to keep me there. I can't show off or be bossy. I can't rock the boat 'cause I ain't the only one in the boat."

He snapped the hubcap back on the tire and stood. He put her flat tire and car jack in her trunk and closed the lid, and nodded. "You need to get that flat tire fixed." He shrugged. "Might be for the best, and since you and I are talking kind of open-like, I'd suggest you get a new tag on this car. A Massachusetts tag stands out, and some people don't like to see things around here they are not used to seeing. Causes suspicion. It's sort of unusual for you to be here anyway, an I know what you are doing here is your business and all, but folks won't notice as much if you change the tag."

She nodded. "I've been thinking the same thing. Good advice. Anyway, you're Sam to me, and any time you want to call me Cleo, I'd like that too." She looked over at his truck. "That's an old truck you've got there."

He turned to give his truck an appraisal. "Well, used to be, I'd pick up workers and bring them to the mill and park over by the hotel every day."

"Hotel?"

He gave a forced laugh. "Cordray's Mill was bigger in the thirties and on into the forties through the war. It took a lot of people to help with the farming, and in those days, there was a hotel over by the lake, near where Mister John puts his boat in now, but it burned down. The dance hall was full many a night, not just on Saturdays or holidays. Over at the dance hall, they had that colored fella I told you about with a band that used to play for folks to dance in towns all around here."

"Dancing for white people, you mean."

"Band got paid, folks got to dance, and everybody was happy." He bowed his head, then gave her a final look. "I understand what you are saying to me. Things will change, and the sooner, the better. But in the meantime, we all got to live around here. Come on and follow me back to the mill. I'll keep an eye out for you in case something else goes wrong."

Let's Dance

Joyce Cordray called Cleo to come over for coffee. When they were settled, Joyce said, "I want to thank you for the idea."

Cleo looked puzzled. "Idea?"

"Well, Sam told me you had been talking about our little community and asking about its past. Anyway, he told me how you liked the stories about when we used to have dances here. I got to thinking and decided that maybe if we tried to do that again, it might bring more people here, to dance … but also to shop at the store, buy our grits and corn meal and such. Even go fishing with John. We need to do something to kick some life into this place, and that might just do it."

Cleo shook her head. "Well, I didn't think of all that."

"Yes, but you have a fresh perspective. I've been thinking for some time that we needed to invest in this place to give it a chance to pick up again. I can't afford to do much, but this dance thing is worth a try. I think it's a right smart idea." Joyce softened her look at Cleo in a motherly way. "Just your being here has made me think of things I might not have otherwise. My husband used to say, take the credit when you can. So, congratulations to you. Anyway, I've asked Sam and John to clean up around here and try to get the pool up to being used again. John can see to the repairs to make sure the pavilion is up to snuff. It might take us getting someone for over in Albany to get the mold and algae out of the pool."

Cleo looked out the window and across the yard at the store and pavilion, "I hope it works and is successful. This is a pretty place. It deserves to have more people around to enjoy it." After she made the comment, Cleo thought to herself that if more people started to come here, she might have to move on to a quieter hiding spot.

Joyce followed Cleo's glaze absentmindedly. "Anyway, we might have to use the barn where your car is parked for storing some things and such. I'll tell Sam and John to work around it or to find a covered place on the side just for you to park."

Cleo felt a chill up her back. She had intended to find a better hiding place for the suitcase and now would have to retrieve it from under some bundles of cloth to which she had recently added and an old saddle. Joyce continued, "Anyway, Carolyn tells me she does not think the idea will work, but I need to try something. She suggested having a disc jockey play records rather than hiring an orchestra or a band to save some money. Maybe she is right about that." They both continued to glance out of the window, one's thoughts on the dance and the other's on the suitcase.

Graham and Wallace

Sam Lloyd was getting a drink of water from the pipe of the flowing well in front of the swimming pool when he saw Graham and Wallace heading toward him carrying their bamboo cane fishing poles and a can of worms from behind Mrs. Cordray's house. "Graham … Wallace, how you young gentlemen doing today?

Graham answered, "We doin just fine, Sam. How's the mill?"

"Mill's mostly taking care of itself. We could use more business, but near about everybody says that."

Wallace, not wanting his brother to dominate the conversation, said, "Y'all selling any of that corn meal or grits you put in the new bags?"

Sam smiled. "I think Mrs. Cordray done hit on a good idea baggin it with that picture of the mill on the sack. We sellin it in the grocery stores over in Albany and some other towns around abouts. Anyway, lots more than Miss Carolyn sells here at the store. What you goin fishing for?"

Graham now reasserted himself. "Anything we can catch. Daddy said he'd cook up whatever we brung home."

Wallace said, "In school, they said to say brought, not brung."

"You so smart, you can carry whatever we catch back home and clean 'em."

Sam calmed them by adding, "Well, with good fishermen like you two around here, there likely ain't likely gonna be anything left in the lake."

Graham shrugged his shoulders. "That's the plan." They walked on past him to the bridge.

He raised his voice as they moved on past. "I may bring my grandson here one day again soon to fish with you. Maybe you can show him some more about how to catch fish."

Wallace answered with a laugh. "Be glad to. Just make sure you send him to me 'cause Graham likes to get his hook hung in a tree limb first thing."

Graham shouted back over his shoulder. "Sam, you know that ain't true."

Sam shouted at them as he walked to the store, "Y'all stay on the bridge. Don't get down in those weeds and step on a snake."

Planning a Party

Cleo brought a fresh pot of coffee onto the porch where she, Joyce, and Carolyn were meeting to discuss the ongoing plans for revitalizing Cordray's Mill. Talmadge slept at Joyce's feet. Once she was seated, the conversation resumed.

As Carolyn explained her idea to paint the store and mill with bright colors, both Cleo and Joyce Cordray began to find more and more objections. Realizing she was being outvoted, Carolyn interrupted their conversation by changing the subject. She suddenly leaned back in her chair with a surprised expression on her face. "Did you read what was in the paper about that Boston Brinks Robbery? Cleo, you must have heard." With no response, Carolyn renewed her latest point of conversation with more facts. "They finally caught some more of the gang that broke into that Brink's depository." She looked at Cleo, who had a surprised look on her face. Now becoming frustrated that no one was picking up on her desire to talk about something else other than the revitalization plans, Carolyn leaned forward and continued. "The robbery happened several years ago, back when you were still living there. Don't you remember?"

Cleo blinked. "I do remember when it happened. It was in all the news at the time."

Now feeling she had some traction, Carolyn sniffed and continued. "Well, they caught several of them, and one lady died from being beaten to tell them where she had hidden the money. Seems like she was a girlfriend of one of the robbers. They never did find the money. It said in the paper they are looking for people that may have left town with the rest of the money. Both the police and the outlaws!" Cleo set her cup down gently and walked away to the edge of the porch to look out at the lake. This action just made Carolyn talk louder so she could hear, and she leaned forward toward Cleo. "No telling how many more of them are out there. Wonder if they will try to break these guys out of jail that were just caught? Maybe they will start to turn on each other and fight among themselves or start killing each other? No telling what the police will do."

Joyce Cordray sat her coffee cup down emphatically, which drew Carolyn up. The action also awakened Talmadge, who lifted his head and looked around. "Carolyn, you just have too vivid an imagination. Let's stick to what we all got together to discuss. We gotta dance to plan. Can't you see this kind of talk is distracting Cleo from her ideas?"

Swimming Pool

The next week, between John, Sam, and the swimming pool company from Albany, the concrete blocks covering the former wooden pool, were patched, made watertight, cleaned, and declared fit for use.

After a thorough scrubbing of the pool, water from the nearby lake was pumped into it, and filtered to keep out the larger bits of pond debris. Although it was warmed by the sun, the water temperature was still cool, and the difference between it and the air temperature was usually considerable. However, it did not take long for the word to spread, and local moms and kids, as well as gawky teenagers, soon were splashing in the pool. All the local mothers of small kids were excited about this new diversion from the boredom of southwest Georgia in the mid-1950s. After a dip, they sat on the sides of the pool, swinging their legs through the water to keep their circulation going.

The influx of visitors did have the intended consequences, and Carolyn was selling more food, drinks, and gas from the store. She was beginning to admit the idea was not so bad after all. The only negative reaction was from Carolyn's cat, Roscoe. All the strangers coming in and out of the store made her nervous, and she stayed out of sight.

Although Cleo, for the past several weeks, had mostly entertained herself sequestered among the few buildings and scattered residents that constituted Cordray's Mill, she longed for a social outing and conversation with other young women her age. She and John had visited and talked, but his boys were always nearby, and then he had to be at their home to feed them, help them with their homework, get them to bed, and then off to school the next day. Both she and John felt there was not much time to be by themselves. Listening to the noise across the street, she thought to herself that she might make some friends over at the pool, and they would help her pass the time more agreeably. Besides, it was likely that many of the people now talking and laughing across the street would come to the dance when it happened on the coming weekend, and maybe she could make some friends now for that social occasion.

She looked through her wardrobe and found the one-piece bathing suit she had purchased with the other new clothes in Richmond. She held it up, pleased with herself. It was the latest thing in European fashion. In her excitement to belong and to make a good first impression, she did not think how different this bathing suit was from the ones people were used to seeing in the vicinity of Cordray's Mill. This was not a bathing suit with layered frills about the breast line and a tennis skirt bottom. This was a fabric that was thin and with few lines that showed where the stretchy cloth was sewn together. This was like a second skin over a first skin that was primeval. This was to show what women were supposed to look like. This was a bathing suit that shouted, "Mama, get the calf rope, I'm heading for Satan." Cleo had a figure that could stop a train.

After she slid it on and adjusted the edges, she grabbed a towel from the bathroom and walked in her sandals across the street to the noise of splashing and laughter. As she approached the swimming pool, she noticed the noise level decline and then stop altogether by the time she reached the pool's edge. She smiled and nodded at people, at the women with their kids gathered nearby watching her approach. Some politely smiled back. The noise and conversation, however, had dropped to a whisper, an all-time low for the mid-day gathering. Cleo, feeling nervous and without anyone to engage with in conversation and not knowing what to expect from the throng of visitors, jumped into the pool. The water was shockingly icy, and when she quickly emerged, she felt the cold had caused the thin, clinging fabric to make her more noticeable, in certain places. She quickly grabbed the towel and wrapped it around her, but not before most of the people, particularly the teenage boys on that side of the pool, received an indelible memory.

There were introductions and some polite conversation that followed, but the mood of the visiting ladies that day had been firmly fixed, and no discussion of dance music or the ingredients of finger sandwiches could reset the atmosphere.

Union Station

After a two-days crunched into the stiff seats and one night bouncing in a Pullman sleeper car, the two sleepy, grumpy men changed trains in Atlanta for the last leg of the journey on the Central of Georgia railroad from Atlanta to Albany. They finally pulled into the Union station a short distance from the banks of the Flint River.

Climbing slowly down onto the platform, they walked stiffly and stopped to stretch by luggage carts with metal-rimmed carriage wheels spun silver smooth by use. Soon one of these carts would pull the crate of material they had shipped with them marked "tractor parts" along the siding of the tracks and into the Railway Freight office for distribution.

They found the ticket office and waited for the luggage to be processed by sitting on the long wooden benches spaced with armrest dividers to prevent reclining sleepers. Looking around, they were surprised at the high ceilings both on the freight platform with its arched access corridors as well as inside the ticket offices. Then one of them, impatient with the slow progress, called on the pay phone to the local auto dealer who had agreed to rent them a used car for the week. Back in Boston, they had calculated that a car with a Georgia tag and perhaps local decals bolstering high school sporting teams would be less conspicuous than driving down in a car from Massachusetts. The person at the dealership promised that someone

116

would bring them the car in the next hour and pick up the rental payment. The man looked at his watch and sighed.

The other man went to check at the Railway Freight office about the crate of material they had brought with them. He noticed the street in front of the station, named Roosevelt Street, was made from red bricks stretching as far as he could see in a straight line to the west. He tried to imagine the work involved in laying brick streets by hand, one at a time. He noticed a GMC truck dealership on Washington Street just to the right of Roosevelt with a sign on the front that read Beck Motor Company.

While they were waiting for the car to be delivered, they checked their luggage in a locker and were directed by the ticket agent to walk up to Washington Street and turn left to reach Hubble's Restaurant. By the time they got back from lunch, the car had been delivered, and they retrieved the luggage and the crate of goods from the freight office. They decided to wait until they were in a more private location to open the crate, which contained some clothes wrapped around several guns and ammunition to keep the metal from clanking when the crate was moved.

As they drove away from the depot on the brick streets, one man said to the other, "I wasn't expecting everything to look this new around here, but it sure is slow as hell."

The other looked around and nodded, "I remember reading that they had a bad tornado about fifteen years ago that tore up the town pretty good, and I guess they had to rebuild a bunch of it. Still, there is just a bunch of hicks living here."

After consulting a road map, even as tired as they were, they decided to make a dry run and drove to the town of Morgan, about 35 miles away. As they passed through Cordray's Mill about five miles before they reached Morgan, they were surprised at how little there was to the place. Outside of a store with a gas pump and a mill building on the creek bank, there were only a few houses. There was a sign in front of a pavilion advertising a coming dance. As they passed over the curving bridge by the mill, they kept looking for more signs of a town. Then they made a loop to return to Albany through the nearby town of Leary so they would not look suspicious riding on the one road through Cordray's Mill too often.

As they left Morgan and moved east toward Leary, one man snapped his fingers and said, "I didn't think of something till now."

"What's that?"

"These folks round here don't talk like we do?"

"What ya mean?"

"Remember how that fella at the train station and the restaurant looked at us when we talked to them? We stick out like a sore thumb. It's our accents."

"Well, maybe we just try to talk like they do here."

"Are you kidding me? That won't work."

"Maybe we should act like we had a sore throat?"

"Both of us?"

"How about we were foreigners? Remember in the war how those folks tried to speak English? Maybe that would work if we tried to sound Italian."

"Hell, the Italians were against us in the war.

And, what if we ran into someone who really did speak Italian, and they started to talk to us in that jibber?"

"Maybe we could be Scottish or Irish or something like that ... maybe from Sweden?"

"Mmmm. Let's think about that. Just seems like anything we do will likely draw attention to ourselves."

"Hell, let's just find this bitch, get the money and shoot her. We ain't gonna take up residence down here."

"Naw. We need to think this through. Can't just go in and shoot everybody there. We need a plan."

Pavilion

As John DuVall scrubbed himself in the shower, he was remembering his earlier days after he had returned from the war and his times at the local honky-tonks. It was in one of those raucous places where he had met his wife. He could still picture those noisy bars where the parking lots were covered with crushed beer cans and bottle caps. On the edges of the dance floor and in the back of the parking areas, the local toughs lurked with straight razors, or brass knuckles kept shallow in their pants pockets. He remembered the implied threats in the atmosphere from those pretending to be badasses were in such a contrast to what he had seen when he was in uniform. Those were the lonely days of missing his mother when his soul was also still wounded over the war.

He also remembered the cheap cologne smell of the women when he walked in, past the neon signs selling beer. The young women would be smiling, alluring, teasing, twisting back and forth, looking to become a gateway to controversy, hoping to be the one to put one man jammed up against another over her. In addition to recalling the fear, the warning signs, and the hesitation, he still remembered that when he entered right away and without a shadow of a doubt that those were the places he wanted to be.

Toweling off, he looked in the mirror and wished he was taller and had bigger arms. He wished he had a tougher look and was better able to absorb pain. Heart pain was likely where he was he was headed with Cleo, and lots of it. He tried on the other shirt. He tucked it in and turned to the left and right. Graham and Wallace watched from the doorway and nudged each other in the ribs. He then returned to the bathroom to check his hair. The boys followed, grinning.

Graham worked up the courage to say, "You gonna scare the fish shining like that."

Wallace, not to be outdone, added, "You like to step on whoever's feet you dance with. Whoever she might be." Both boys laughed at this.

Their father turned to them, leaned back, and pretended to be miffed. "Don't you worry about me. Just you remember to get to bed by 9:30 and don't be sitting up listening to the music."

Both answered together. "We will."

He gave them another stern look, now leaning towards them. "Don't you dare try to stay up and sneak down to the pavilion, or I'll skin your hides."

They looked at each other first, then said, "We won't."

John looked again in the mirror and thought to himself. *Why didn't I ask her to go with me? I could have gone over to her house and got her and walked her across to the dance. I could have brought her some flowers. He felt there had been mutual interest building between them the past weeks. Now she might think he was not interested. He was so stupid. It was childish of him to be so nervous.*

He looked back at the boys. "You be good now and protect the house."

Both together, "We will."

John took in a deep breath and rolled his eyes.

Earlier that day, as they were finishing hanging the decorations for the dance, Carolyn had told Cleo that she had the remaining work covered and for her to go on home and get ready. Now Cleo watched across the street as Carolyn, with the help of Sam Lloyd, who had closed the mill early, finished the last of the preparations. They had set up the tables and now were hanging the last of the paper lanterns on the support beams along the ceiling by the open sides of the pavilion. As the sun began to drop, when he had finished with the tall work, Sam Lloyd left to drive back to Shellman and his family. Carolyn continued to fuss with the drinks and food and made sure the place for the disk jockey was secured away from the dance floor. She was glad that Joyce had avoided the extra expense of a real orchestra. She could see where earlier Sam had set up Joyce's rocking chair on the front porch, so she, along with Talmadge, could look across the street and watch all the activities.

Later that afternoon, when the music started and drifted across the road through the moss and leaves passing the lightning bugs to her window, Cleo watched as the remains of the sunset reflected on the water. She felt the allure of the place and the promise of being social again. That attraction was balanced by the risk of being recognized or noticed by someone who would say something to somebody who would tell someone else. The road back to Boston was laid with the tracks of peril. Still, she could not live in a hole for the rest of her life.

Cleo pulled back from the window. She needed to get a hold of herself. Surely, she was being overly cautious. She was here and needed to blend in … to be a part of this new environment, at least for a time. This was the place she had chosen to make her feel safe. If she at least didn't go over there and make an appearance, then that would be even more noticeable. After what happened at the swimming pool, she knew the local people must be talking about her. Wondering who she could be. What was her past? Why was she here? She looked in the closet for the dress she had planned to wear.

She was thinking of John as her feet crunched, crunched, crunched on the gravel, and that sound almost gave a rhythm to match the beat of the music as she approached. Why was he being so cautious with her? Maybe it was because he had the boys.

123

As the noise of the music grew louder ahead, she could see that the trucks and cars were nose-to-tail on both sides of the narrow Georgia two-lane road. She could recognize the tags representing people who had driven from Dawson, Leary, Edison, Arlington, and even one from Albany. Inside the pavilion, people were laughing and talking, and some stood on the outside smoking, drinking, and huddled more closely to hear each other's words above the music.

Earlier, John DuVall had passed through the door of the pavilion, past the bar, set up on a folding table where there were several people hanging out, collected there near the whisky, their cigarettes drifting smoke from the ashtrays and quietly talking with the bartender. He could see that Carolyn, Sam, and Cleo had done a presentable job in the decorating. However, as he entered, here inside, the temperature was noticeably hotter and humid enough to start him perspiring immediately. He could see some of the people lined along wooden benches on the sides of the walls, some nervously flirting, and some holding hands in the night.

On the crowded dance floor, it appeared several of the younger boys were hoping to become James Dean with peg pants and rolled-up short sleeves that accented their bearing and their walk, trying their best to look nonchalant. These wannabees were with the younger girls wearing their tight pedal pushers, and shirts with the bottoms tied about the waist. Most of the men here were like him in more regular clothes, not quite what they would have on the next day in church, but much better than the rough-hewn work clothes they normally wore. The wooden dance floor was littered with corn meal allowing the dancers to glide their steps to the music.

Still, as he watched, he felt many of the people here were insecure and awkward, even in this simple social environment - none more so than he was. Even though he had scrubbed himself clean and had on his best shirt and pants, he was palm-sweaty nervous as he stopped to stand and observe along one the side of the pavilion closest to the banks of the flowing water. One of the local Klansmen, Jessie Miles, nearby sneered to his friends and the woman standing by his side when John passed. "That's the guy who can't keep his woman." He remembered seeing Jessie's female companion being overly friendly with him while she watched him at the checkout counter at the Colonial Store when he was buying food. Now she pretended not to notice him. The others with Jessie hardly gave him a sniff.

The only dress Cleo had fit to wear to a dance was a Boston-style dress, more modern and alluring than any of the local ladies in their billowing floral print patterns, long fabrics scraping the floor as though seeking puritanical church approval. The length of her black and white dress was shorter, more like something Marilyn Monroe or Elisabeth Taylor could have pulled off. The top was also fitted like they might have done to attract a leading man. Cordray's Mill was not used to this level of self-confidence.

Outside, the men standing, smoking, and drinking, got quiet as they watched her approach the steps leading up to the dance floor. They parted to give her space and nodded respectfully, although she could tell there was something more personal to the looks than respect. When he saw her enter, John began to maneuver slowly toward the door.

Tonight was the first time she had been in such a large group since she left Boston and the crowd of strangers made Cleo nervous. As she entered, she stood backlit by the door and let her worried eyes sweep left and right in the dimly lit space, searching for undesirable but familiar faces … past him … to the other side. Whoops, was that … no. That was not someone she recognized. Now looking back toward the other side as the music changed to a slower song. She had almost finished searching … frowning.

His heart dropped. She was turning away, looking for something … someone better. From a slight breeze, he could smell the lotion he put on his hair, to make himself up … for her. Now she will only see him as foolish. He looked over at the bar, and a familiar hunger rose in his stomach. She will see his childish longing and need. She will see him as this stupid hick, county.

Her face was turning now, away from the far corners, back to what she was looking for. Back to him. His walk had taken him to

126

within a few feet of her. Too late to move back and not be noticed as coming over to her. Too late not to be obvious.

She smiled at him and said, "So, John, what do I have to do to get you to ask me to dance?"

They moved together, sliding across the cornmeal on the notes of the music toward the lantern lights at the edges of the room by the open walls inviting a breeze from the water. They owned the night. Later, as the music drifted into ballads and still slower dance music, Cleo, with her head on John's shoulder, looked across the water to see Sam's truck parked near the mill.

Cleo and John

It was a rainy school day morning, and as John watched Graham and Wallace get onto the school bus, he hoped that nothing would happen to stop them from staying over in Morgan to study after school with the teacher as he had arranged. Then he came as quietly and as unnoticeably as he could, jogging through the rain to the back door of the cottage and then into Cleo's bed. Later he looked through the almost sheer curtains out in the yard as puddles formed to create small barriers hiding him and protecting them both from the secret romance he and Cleo now shared.

Nothing in his life, in the war, in the heartache and death of his mother, in the shame of his wife leaving, and later, in the frustrations of raising the boys alone, in all the days of pampering obnoxious would-be fishermen back into the draws of the creek, prepared him for what he was feeling with Cleo. All his life's difficulties on one side of the scale could not tip him back from where he was now on that other side. He was golden. He watched her sleeping after they had made love, and there was nothing like it in the world. The past few days had been the best of his life.

She stirred, then stretched, exposing her bare arms above the sheets. Her pale green eyes opened to look at him, and she smiled first, then suddenly, as if a terrible memory rushed into her mind, she frowned.

Alarmed, his face mimicked hers as he leaned over to her. "What is it? What's wrong?"

She gathered the sheets just above her breasts and leaned up to look at him with the concern still fixed. "I'm desperate and need your help. I don't want to drag you into anything bad and dangerous, but don't know who else to turn to."

"I'll help in any way I can. What's wrong?"

"Let me tell it to you from the beginning. It has to do with why I came here and why I'm so scared. I told you earlier that I had worked in a bar in Boston. Well, I made friends with another girl who worked there, and we became roommates. She later got a boyfriend who I had met but didn't know too well, and they were supposed to get married in the spring. He always seemed kind of edgy to me. As time passed, her boyfriend got himself mixed up with a bunch of other people who became criminals. Anyway, this guy she dated was one of the men who robbed the Brinks depository facility. I didn't know anything about what they were doing at the time.

"Afterwards, they had all this money, maybe three million dollars, from robbing that Brinks building in north Boston. It was a big deal when it happened and was in all the papers. I read later that it took the gang's leaders years to plan. Anyway, after the robbery, they did not split up the money. Instead, they hid it for several years. I don't understand why they did that. These guys just went back to work or whatever like nothing had happened. The police continued to look for them, and as time passed, they started to catch some of them.

"Anyway, the police were getting hot on the trail of these men. So, this guy … he gave my friend a suitcase to hold for him and to hide. Well, this guy and his friends got very jumpy every time I was around them when they came to see her. I don't know what happened, but one time, I came home, and she was there on the floor all beat up. I took her to the hospital, but she had this blood thing where they couldn't stop her from bleeding. In the hospital, she told me all about it and said these men were starting to turn on each other and were cleaning up loose ends, or something like that. The doctors said they couldn't do anything for her. She was a sweet girl; just was bad at picking men. She told me they'd be coming after me next cause they suspected my friend had the suitcase and they knew me. She said to get it and go as far away as I could.

"I got scared and just did it. I set it up with Mrs. Cordray's granddaughter, the one I had met from a couple of years ago. No one from Boston would ever think of looking in South Georgia for me and all the money. So, I left Boston and didn't tell anyone where I was going. I just disappeared. I picked it up on the way out of town and didn't even open the suitcase to see what was in it till I hit Richmond. It's all that money from the Brink's job from a few years ago that they never found. I've counted it, and it's about two and a half million dollars. I took out a big handful which should be enough last me a couple of years if I don't flash it.

"I was not a part of that robbery in any way and was just as shocked about it as everyone else. But, when I followed my roommate's advice and took that suitcase and looked inside, I was in it as much as any of them.

"Now, those bad men are looking for me, and so are the cops. If they come here and find me, they'll go through everything I have. I think if I don't have all that money with me, I could convince them I left town cause I was scared and just wanted to get away. That's the only way I can survive. I'm way out here alone on a limb, and everyone has a saw."

John shook his head. "I don't care what you did or didn't do, but I'll do what I can to help."

"Oh, John. Thank you. You are the only person I can depend on."

"Well, I ain't much to count on. I'm kinda … what you see is what you get, and that ain't much compared to you. You know … you are … much more of a person who stands out than me. You are strong and decisive, not to mention beautiful. I'm not sure what you see in me. I'm not that strong. I don't know how I can stack up to you. I know you will probably leave here as soon as you can. I'll help, but I'm asking, please don't give my boys any ideas of something else. Don't get their hopes up."

Cleo reached one hand to the side of his cheek. "Don't run yourself down. You are solid. You are not full of the bluster and grab ass that I've seen in so many men. There is this false cockiness in most men that I've seen in bars and just in life generally. So many men just want to get what they can out of you before all the pretty goes away. You don't try to make yourself out to be like some kind of movie star. You shine from the inside out. There is something in those other kinds of men that feels desperate. You are better than that. You are the real thing. I look at you, and I see a stable life. I see honesty and good character. I see those boys growing up and getting married and having kids of their own. I see a real life, not some fancy, glitter-filled rocket ship. Don't ever think you are not the person I want to be with. You're everything I want to be with. While we are at it, what about your hopes? What do you want in the future?"

John shook his head carefully so as not to dislodge her hand on his cheek. "I'm in kind of shock over all of this ... you ... you being here ... what you told me. The idea that I can be here in bed with you. I don't want to wake up from this dream. What I hope is to never wake up. Anything else is gravy."

Cleo reached up with her other hand to bracket his face, "First, we've got to do something about the money."

Armageddon

The two men from Boston headed to Hubble's Restaurant for lunch. One of them was wiping his face with a damp cloth. The other said to him, "Where the hell did you go last night?"

The other wadded up the cloth and tossed it out the window of the car. "I figured because it was near about our last night here, I'd go out to the Black Cat nightclub. Wanted to see if that little lady was going to be back there."

"You find her?"

"Yeah. That's why my face is so puffy this morning. It was a late night. I was kind of celebrating."

"You oughtn't to have done that. We got our main business to take care of soon. You don't want anyone here remembering you."

"Don't worry. Yesterday afternoon, I took that truck we rented for the day and stopped for gas at the filling station they got down there. Got a look at the lay of the land. Good thing is, that fat old lady that runs the store is a talker. I acted like I had a sore throat and could only talk in a whisper and pointing , but I didn't say much at all. She let it slip that a strange woman is renting the small house in the back of the bigger one across the street. That fits with what the waitress in the bar back in Boston found out from the college girl. Her car's in the barn over to the side of the yard. That is what I was celebrating."

"Well, good. We got our target."

"She also said that the woman who owns all that land around there, Mrs. Cordray was hard up and needed money."

"To make this work clean, we need to get that old lady who owns the big house away from there. Maybe we could call her and say we were investors down here in Albany looking to buy some land and wanted to see her about the property she owns. Something like that. That would get her attention, get her to leave and come over come here to meet with us on the land, and it'd also cover our accents. We could tell her to come over here to Albany at a certain time, and then go over to get the money at the same time. It'd take her a couple hours to figure it was not real and get back there. By that time, we'd have done with that Cleo gal, have the money, and be gone."

"Yeah. Tell her to bring that store lady. Tell that Cordray lady it would help to convince us that having that other lady running the store would be a benefit to us after we made the investment. That would get both of them out of there at the same time."

John watched Carolyn drive Joyce Cordray away for a meeting they had over in Albany. Carolyn had put a sign on the store and one by the pool that both were closed for the day. John herded his kids over to the place where the boat was docked on the shore. There they met Sam Lloyd, who had brought his grandson to work with him that day.

John looked his boys back, and forth and at Sam's grandson also. "Boys, I got to help Sam here with fixing something in the mill today. Neither one of us want you all running around and getting in our way or playing in the road out here." He pointed. "So, Wallace and Graham, while I'm helping Sam over at the mill, you boys take the boat with Sam's grandson. Use the oars, and don't mess with the motor. You all wear the life vests ALL THE TIME. Just row it using both paddles up along the side of the lake. I want you all to surprise Sam and me with what you catch. Don't go up too far. Don't go out in the deep part, and don't get out of sight of the road down here wherever you go."

The three boys looked at each other excitedly and made a move toward the boat. "Wait. Let me get my tackle box out. You don't need that, and you got the worms for the cane poles. That's all you need for this morning anyway." John got his tackle box out of the boat, and the boys pushed off, each wanting to have a turn at the oars.

John and Sam smiled at each other as they watched the boys intent on fishing and struggling with the oars as the boat zig-zagged across the water. Then they turned toward the mill, and a problem that involved adjusting the gears that turned the stones.

Earlier that day, the men from Boston cleared out of the hotel, loaded their suitcases and the guns, and headed to Cordray's Mill. Now the men watched by the side of the road. There was a sign on the door that the store was closed for the day. They took that to mean that the lady from the store and the one in the house had both gone to Albany together. They slowly rolled down the car windows. As they watched and listened, the door to the mill was open, and there was some faint noise from activity there, but it was all coming from the inside.

Everything else was still and quiet. There was some slight noise of irregular bumping coming from up the lake, but it was far away. Satisfied, they pulled off the road further into the edge of the yard in front of the big house. They could not see anyone around to stop them from their business with Cleo.

Cleo was alerted from her ironing by a slight sound that raised her alarm. She turned to see a man coming toward her porch. She did not recognize him but instantly felt by the look on his face that he was one of them. She moved quickly to run out the back door, but there was another man there carrying a shotgun. Her heart sank. Time had run out. They had found her. She was as good as dead. They all were.

As one man entered the back door of her small rental cottage, Cleo ran out the front, dodged the man coming up the steps, and headed toward the barn. She had only gone about ten paces when the man grabbed her suddenly from behind and pointed a pistol at her. She stopped still. The other man arrived, and they both looked her up and down. "Get her back in there." Inside the house, they threw her down on the couch.

"Where's the money?"

She tried to tamp down the fear and swallowed. "I'm afraid I don't know what you are talking about. I don't know who you are or why you are here."

One man immediately backhanded her and said to the other. "Watch her ass. This ain't much of a place. Money can't be too hard to find." He sat a shotgun he was holding down, on the counter next to the sink and began to rummage through the cabinets in the kitchen and then in the one bedroom throwing open doors and drawers.

Cleo dabbed her bleeding lip with the collar of her shirt. She listened to the banging in the bedroom and heard the anger of the man, who was growing increasingly frustrated. The man returned red-faced and picked up the shotgun. The other man near her said, "She was headed out toward that barn. Must be where it is and not in here."

The other said, "Yeah, well it sure ain't here. Let's take her to the barn where she has her car and get the money " As they walked quickly with the men half pulling her, Cleo struggled to break free, but the man held her too tightly. They continued to maneuver her toward the barn, with her struggling, pushing, and pulling away from them all the time.

As they wrestled her into the barn, one of the men holding a shotgun leaned it against the wall next to an array of farm implements. The man who was not holding her arms slapped her across her lips again. It was all she could do not to fall. "Okay lady, you know why we're here. Get the cash, or we're gonna start cutting you up. Don't play stupid. We know who you are, and we know you got it."

He grabbed her by one arm and told the other man, "Gimmie me that hunting knife and leave that door cracked so I can see in here." When they had dragged her in, Cleo had kicked up the dust that was in a cloud around them. Careful to hold the knife in one hand, he waved his hand at his face because of the dust, and it took a moment for all of them to adjust their eyes to the dim lighting in the barn. He used the sharp blade to cut off her apron held by the straps over her neck. As it fell to the dirt, he looked her up and down and ran his hands along her body. "Damn, Girlie, if we weren't in such a hurry, I might have to spend some time with you in this barn. Now, tell me where you got that money hid, or I'm gonna start with your face and cut you up and down."

138

The other man ripped the tarp off the car sitting in the middle of the dirt floor still with the Massachusetts tag. That action kicked up another blast of dust. When it finally settled enough, they could see that other than the car,, most of what was in the barn was just a bunch of farm junk. There seemed to be dust everywhere on all the tools and farm implements hanging on the walls and scattered on the floor. As one man continued to threaten Cleo with the knife, the other man put the pistol he was holding in his belt to use both hands to move things around the barn in his search for the suitcase. He began kicking over farm materials, boxes, and bags. Then he said hopefully, "I can see where something was dragged over here by these croaker sacks. It's got be in here somewhere."

When he came out of the mill to get a breath of fresh air, John noticed the strange car parked on the lawn of Mrs. Cordray's house. He had become extra suspicious of strangers since Cleo told him the real reason of the threat from Boston. When he looked closer, her screen door was open and slightly off the hinges and the barn door was ajar. That was enough to kick his adrenalin into high gear.

He shouted inside. "Sam get out here! I need your help but be careful." Run up the side of the lake and make sure the boys stay back up there. I think that bad man from Boston is here to hurt Cleo, and I gotta stop him." He pulled his gun out of the tackle box, checked to see that it was fully loaded, and looked over at the barn. "It might be more than one of them. What's gonna happen may get bad, Sam, real bad." He took off in a dead run for the barn.

The man with the knife was running the dull side up and down Cleo's cheek, not cutting her yet, just scaring her. "I said, where is it? Your face don't have to get all messed up over a few dollars. Where —" John crashed through the doors into the barn and ran, gun in hand, toward the men. As they both turned to John, he instinctively shot the one with the pistol in his belt as the man reached for the gun. The man froze with a surprised look on his face, then fell to the ground like a puppet whose strings had been cut.

The other man quickly pushed Cleo aside and jumped at John, grappling with him to get his gun. In making his move to grab John's gun, he dropped the knife he had been holding on Cleo. However, he was bigger and stronger than John, and was rapidly taking over control of John's hand holding the gun. He threw John to the dirt. As he was picking up the gun and turning it into the palm of his hand for control, Cleo, now free from his grasp, spun and grabbed a pitchfork leaning against the wall. She stabbed him in his back just below his shoulders. He shrieked, winced, and with his knees buckling, began to turn to her, painfully grabbing for his back, and his grip on the gun went slack. She pulled out the pitchfork and stabbed him again with all her might burying all four of the long thin tines of the pitchfork deep into his belly. The man went down, moaning. She did it again, hitting him higher in his chest and grunting with the effort. As she began to pull it out to strike him once more, John stopped her and retrieved the gun from the man's lifeless hand.

After checking on the boys, Sam arrived at the barn to find the dust still unsettled in the air floating over the two men who lay still, one with a pitchfork leaning out of his body at an odd angle and bouncing slowly in the air. John had a hand on Cleo, who was leaning against the wall staring at the bodies. She put a hand over her face and began to weep and pressed herself further into the wall as if she was trying to get away.

John turned to Sam and quickly re-told the story of the crazy Boston suitor who would not leave Cleo alone. Sam looked at John, sensing the faults in the story John was telling nervously about the boyfriend. Sam could tell there was more to what had just happened than an angry boyfriend. The danger that was now on all of them was much bigger than that. Cleo was shaking and crying softly as John finished the boyfriend story. Then it became quiet as the dust continued to settle, and all three of them looked at the bodies.

As the one most distant to the emotions in the air, Sam spoke, "Whatever we gonna do here, we need to decide before Mrs. Cordray and Miss Carolyn both get back.

Cleo snapped out of her shock. "We gotta hide it all. If anybody finds out, they'll be more of them coming."

John nodded in agreement. "She's right, Sam. You gotta help us by not saying anything to anybody." They all looked down at the bodies.

Sam took a deep breath and said, "I speck you askin me a heap more than that." He looked in the direction of the lake and then reached out to close the barn door completely. "We gotta think about them boys out there. No matter what, we all in this together now."

John nodded at Cleo. "He's right. Sam, you take the boys in your truck to Morgan and get them some ice cream. Keep them over there. I got some cleaning up to do here."

Sam leaned forward slightly and said with emphasis. "No sir." That stopped John and Cleo, who looked at him. Sam looked around some more and held out a hand in a stop motion. "Hold on Mister John. Let's think about what we got here. We need to split up and get these chores done soon 'fore the ladies get back here, or somebody drops by to visit.

"Now I'm going to bringing my truck over here." He pointed toward the yard outside. "John, get everything out of that car; those men came in papers, clothes, anything - put it in the back of my truck. Our church got a yard sale this weekend. I'll put their clothes in it. By next week they'll be scattered all over four counties. I'll throw the guns and all else into the lake and burn any papers."

Sam then looked at her. "Miss Cleo, you need to pull yourself together. Stop crying. John and I will push your car outside. Go and change that shirt you have on to something that ain't got blood on it, and put some ice on that lip.

"When I go to get the truck, I'll call for the boys to row back here from fishing. I'm gonna tell them it was the sound of a car backfiring on the road in case the boys heard that shot. Miss Cleo, you hurry. Get your keys and drive your car over and cross the yard to where the boat is docked. Meet the boys there when they get to the boat dock, and then you take them outta here to town for the ice cream."

Then he turned, "Mister John, you need to get rid of that car they come in. Ain't nobody gonna stop you if you were pulling it behind your truck. If I was to try, they'd stop me thinking I stole it. You need to pull it someplace far off and then park it where there won't be any questions leading back to here."

He looked down at the floor. "I'll talk care of these gentlemen here in the barn. I know what to do, and it won't matter if I get all dirty."

As Cleo was loading the boys in her car to take them for ice cream, Sam helped John hook the car the men had driven on a short chain close to the rear of John's truck, and Sam watched John pull it in tandem behind his truck out onto the road.

After both of them had driven away, Sam put the bodies in the back of his pickup and, with a rake, stirred the dirt in the barn to hide any blood on the ground. Then he drove the bodies to the far side of the mill by the water. He pulled the truck over to the edge near the fast-flowing water below the dam. He tossed in the guns the men had with them. Then he took his pocketknife and punched holes in the chest and stomach of both men so they wouldn't float and pushed them into the middle of the creek downstream from the waterfall where the water was running fast.

He was confident the steam would take them on down to the swamp area. He knew there weren't any roads leading down to the creek for several miles. You couldn't even see the creek again from a car till it crossed the Leary Road down near Morgan. He figured the way the creek twisted and turned through the swamp that was about eight or nine miles. That distance would give a lot of space for those fish, turtles, gators, and buzzards to work on the bodies. There wouldn't be much that looked like a person by the time anyone might run across whatever was left to wash up downstream. He doubted if even any piece of them would ever turn up. Then he washed the blood out of the back of the truck with several buckets of creek water.

When John returned later, he told Sam, "I towed that car of theirs behind my truck on down that road that nobody hardly ever travels outside of harvest time. Had to go slow and steady to keep it smooth. Took it up highway 45, almost to US 82 west of Dawson. I left it where anyone riding on the US highway might see it about a hundred yards back down the county road. Lots of kids on that road coming to and from there on the school bus and other folks going into town. Left the keys in the ignition, and the car unlocked. Wiped it down good. That's gonna be too much of a temptation. Someone will get in and drive it off, and no telling where it will finally turn up. Don't know any way it will be tracked back to here."

Settled Dust

The next day John and Sam avoided looking at each other, both still shocked and shamed by the secrets and violence of the day before and afraid they would be caught and punished for their actions. They were jumpy and watched as cars passed and listened for reports on the radio or to any conversations that might be about missing strangers or found cars.

Joyce Cordray noticed the quiet and distance. She tried to engage Cleo and John about the wild goose chase she and Carolyn had the day before over in Albany to see the men who were making an offer on some land, but never turned up at the meeting place. She thought it a little strange when both John and Cleo would change the subject or find some excuse to leave and seemed almost uninterested in what had happened to her. It was uncharacteristic of both of them not to engage her or listen to a story he had to tell. Even Carolyn's retelling, with her embellishments, could not hold their attention. It seemed strange. Also, even Sam, who usually came over to check on them, was distant.

Later that afternoon, John let her know he was taking a day off to go over to Albany with Cleo and the boys. This also was unusual, but she was glad to see all of them acting more like a real family and doing something that was out of the ordinary and a change from the mundane life around the mill. Sam closed the mill early and left without saying goodnight, which was uncharacteristic of him, but she thought everyone deserved a day to themselves.

She was glad the next day when she got to watch John, Cleo, and the boys drive away on the trip to Albany. Maybe that would get them out of the doldrums and put some spark back into their step.

Moving

It was a lucky coincidence that the need to escape from probing conversations in Cordray's Mill happened just as Cleo had been planning a trip to watch a movie being made. Two weeks before, Cleo learned there was a film being shot about a short hair Basenji dog near Albany with veteran Hollywood character actors Phil Harris and Walter Brennan. She found out how guests could come and watch the filming in the woods and had been planning the trip with John and the boys. Because they would likely be leaving soon, she moved up their schedule. She thought watching a move being made would broaden the boy's horizons. The movie, "Goodbye My Lady," also started the childhood star, blond-haired, lanky Brandon deWilde, who earlier had been in the popular western movie, "Shane," and a relatively unknown black actor, Sidney Poitier.

Now, so soon after the shocking reality of the men from Boston, she and John both felt everyone needed a dose of fantasy and escape to clear the air and the tension between them. On the drive back from visiting the set in the woods, Graham and Wallace were still keyed up from seeing the shorthair Basenji dog. The boys could not get over a dog that did not bark but was good at hunting, and they raved about it all the way home.

When they arrived and were sitting in the front room of Cleo's house, John said, "You know boys, what we saw over on that movie set shows there is a lot more about life than we have here in Calhoun County. There are lots of things even more interesting than that dog."

As they had planned, then Cleo took over the conversation. "Your dad's right. What you saw where they were making that movie is just a little of what is going on out there in the world. We ... your dad and I thought you might like to see it and might want to see more of what's going on out there."

Graham and Wallace were sitting on the couch, quietly facing their father and Cleo. They were nervous and could tell something was up. They had noticed both their father and Cleo had seemed a little quiet and sad all day. John cleared his throat. "Boys, what if we were to move away from here and lived someplace else?"

Wallace, puzzled, asked, "Like over in Morgan where we go to school?"

"Maybe even further. We could come back here to visit any time you wanted to, but we'd be living much further away."

Both boys looked over at Cleo.

John continued. "And Miss Cleo could be with us ... would be joining us."

Cleo unclenched her hands and quickly added, "We were just wondering what you might think about that?"

John quickly added. "We're just talking among ourselves here. No need to tell anyone else."

Cleo continued. "We could get a nice house, and you could go to a good school. You would have lots of other kids your age to play with, and all of us could go on vacations to fun places. You could have bicycles."

Graham asked. "Like Florida? Tommy at school told me they have alligator farms and a house where you go in and can lean over at a crazy angle like you were going to walk up the walls."

Cleo smiled at him. "Yes, like that. I even know of places where they have big caves, and picture shows right there in the same town. We could even go to a major league baseball game."

Wallace looked at Graham and said, "Wow."

Graham added. "Boy, I can't wait to tell my friends at school."

John quickly added. "Not yet. We're just talking secretly among ourselves for now. It may be soon, but let's think about it, and we'll talk in a few days. If you still like the idea, we can start to make plans, but for now, promise not to say anything to anybody."

Cleo and Sam

As Sam was packing his truck to leave for the day, Cleo walked over to the mill. Sam noticed her coming but bowed his head as though he had not seen her. He did not want to talk to her and dredge up the incident in the barn. He closed the tailgate and made a move to get into the cab of the truck as she approached.

Cleo felt his discomfort and raised her voice to stop him. "Sam, you know this has been hard on all of us."

He stopped and took a deep breath looking at the tailgate. "I know, but with you and Mister John, if the law around here found out, they'd likely not do too much to you two for defending yourselves from those Boston folks coming here to hurt you." He turned to look at her. "With me ... to do what I did to white men, that would be different."

She stepped toward him. "But you were just trying to help us, and we were all in shock and not thinking clearly."

"That don't matter. I crossed a line. And every day when I see you and John, I see it all again real clear."

She wiped her hands on her dress. "Well, I wanted to tell you we may be leaving soon, and you won't have us here to remind you, and when we leave, all that taint of the men will go with us. We haven't said anything to Joyce or Carolyn yet, but that's the plan."

He sighed and nodded.

She put a hand on the truck. "I just wanted to tell you in case we did not get the chance, that what you did to help ... we'll both always appreciate it."

He lifted his head and looked at her. "I know that you and John are good people. It's just ... well, maybe what you are doing, you know, to leave will be for the best."

She dropped her hand and took a step back. "Maybe we can come back someday in a year or two when all of us are more settled and can have a proper visit."

"Yes'm. Lord willing, we'll all still be here." He patted the tailgate.

The Fair

As they were finalizing the plans to leave, both John and Cleo looked for ways to get away from Cordray's Mill and the memories of the men from Boston. It was a cool night. John, Cleo, and the boys drove over to Albany to see the regional SOWEGA fair. Cleo learned that the acronym for the fair was derived from a contraction of SOuthWEst GeorgiA. It sounded to her strangely like a cross between an Indian name and a pig squealing. After parking and a walk across the sawdust, they started the visit with a trip to the agricultural exhibits. The boys were amazed at the size of the pigs and cattle. Cleo was amazed by the smell. The boys pointed at the enormous vegetables and the baked and canned goods that had been awarded various colored ribbons and had to be restrained from touching them.

The real draw, however, was the tent-lined fairway with the swirling rides that, with few restraints, zoomed at what seemed like amazingly dangerous speeds. They walked up and down the aisles of games and rides, looking at everything and sampling many of the more intriguing challenges. They threw balls at bottles and picked a yellow plastic duck out of a small flowing stream with the hopes it would have the name of a prize written on the bottom. They shot BBs and threw darts at balloons. John smashed a big mallet into a plate that forced a ball to rise into the air to try to hit a gong, with disappointing results. They hurried past the freak show with weird people cavorting on the stage, some looking like they had alligator skin or two heads. They also quickly turned in another direction when they approached what was called a hoochie coochie show. The boys kept looking back in the direction of both these adventures long past being pulled away.

The rides were the most fun. They ate cotton candy and breaded hot dogs on sticks slathered with mustard. They enjoyed the Ferris wheel and several other adventures with more speed and torque. Still, Wallace got sick and threw up from spinning up, down, and around on the Bullet.

As she guided them through the fairway from booth to booth, one arm on each boy's shoulder, Graham had a feeling like they were related somehow. When a loud noise sounded from across the fairway, Wallace, younger and more sensitive, reached up to grab Cleo's hand. She smiled and held it tighter. Later, he and Wallace talked, and both agreed that one of the best things for them during the trip to the fair was that they were like a real family.

They held hands, kidded each other, and laughed. They scuffed the sawdust on the ground as they walked, kicking up dust that covered their sneakers. In between the rides, they also talked more about moving away soon and living in a larger town, and they wondered together what that would be like. At one of the game places, John won dolls for the boys, but because they were boys, they didn't want a doll, so they got felt cowboy hats instead - one blue and

154

one green with the name SOWEGA Fair stitched on the brim. For many years after, those were the hats the boys wore, even after they moved away and even after they had grown much older and they barely fit.

As they were walking from booth to booth, they saw one of the carnival people shouting at some kids and their parents. "Get on out of here, you deadbeats. I got to make a living and don't need and white trash trying to get something for free. You ain't got the money, you ain't paying the game." Cleo walked over to the man with the kids, who must have been the father. He was standing with his head down and made a move to leave, pulling the shocked kids with him. She handed him a $20 bill. "I saw that you dropped this on the ground over there. You better put it back in your pocket before that sleazy man tries to claim it is his. There are better games on the other side of the fairway anyway." She walked away quickly before anyone could comment and moved purposefully away with the boys and John.

The boys napped on the way home, and when they arrived back in Cordray's Mill, they all sat on Cleo's porch, listened to the crickets, watched the fireflies in the trees, and ate ice cream. John sat to one side, and the boys huddled with Cleo, one on each side of her with her arms around their shoulders. Cleo turned her head back and forth, looking at them both. "I want both of you to promise me that as you go on in life, you will always look for ways to be fair. Stand up and be counted when you see something wrong or unjust. You should always look for ways to help others. That is what being a good grownup is about. Promise me."

Both said together, "We will."

John said, "Now, I want each of you to make plans on what you want to take with us when we move. I've got some things to finish up here that I promised to do, and then we can leave. We'll tell Mrs. Cordray and Carolyn when we're ready, but not before. Help us keep it a surprise. We may be going in a day or two, and you need to be ready to pack for our new place." The boys looked over at their father, and they nodded in agreement to his suggestion and at the wonderful adventure ahead of them.

Civil Rights

Cleo and Joyce were sitting in the rocking chairs on the porch drinking iced tea and talking about the news from Little Rock over the integration at their Central High School.

Cleo was hardly listening as she was dreading the conversation she really was there to have. Joyce had given her a reprieve because she was intent on discussing the latest news from the radio. She was saying, "Well, I guess President Eisenhower knows what he is doing sending in those troops. He did lead us to win World War II. I hear it's all they have been talking about over at the courthouse in Morgan. They go out to the cars to get a drink of whiskey and come back more hexed up to complain some more."

Cleo decided she needed to push aside the feelings of guilt and get this conversation behind her. She sat her glass down with a click. "Joyce, I need to tell you something."

Hearing the tone in Cleo's voice, Joyce stopped her rocking and leaned forward with some concern. "What is it, dear?"

The guilt swelled again as she saw the motherly expression on Joyce's face. She looked away from Joyce Cordray and across the yard as she spoke. "I'm sorry, and this will come as a surprise, but John and I have decided to move." Cleo turned her head to look over at the barn and then the mill as she continued to speak. "We've gotten closer in these past weeks and feel the boys need to be in a bigger town or city so they can get a better education. They need to learn things that they are not likely to get in the schools here." She nodded to herself. "We need to get settled before the next school term starts so the boys can adjust." Cleo realized her guilt and nerves had her rambling. She tried to get hold of her emotions as she wadded up her napkin and turned to look back at Joyce. "We really appreciate all you have done for us. Me and John and his boys. I expect they will be over here soon to tell you themselves."

Joyce let out a slow breath as she gathered her thoughts. "Well, I have seen you all together a lot recently." She thought to herself. *Oh my God! These young people are making a mistake jumping into this so quickly. The boys will be scarred even more if John and Cleo split up. Why don't they just say here?* She cleared her throat and said, "But ...where will you go? I just don't understand why you have to leave so fast."

Even though she could tell Cleo was struggling to share her news, she thought. *This will just about kill us now. Cleo represented the promise of a better future, and John was the glue that made everything work here. I don't know how much longer I can hold out. I can see why they want to leave, but it just seems selfish of them somehow.*

Cleo looked down and began to rock again and now sounded more resigned. "I guess all change takes some time to soak in, but down the road, when this is over, everyone will see it was for the best. Here, I'll help clean up." She gathered the pitcher and glasses to take to the kitchen.

As they were going inside, they heard the squeal of brakes on the road. Joyce turned to look. "Wait a minute. What's that going on over at the mill?"

As they watched, a pick-up truck pulled up to the mill, and six men wearing white robes got out of the cab and jumped from the cargo bed. They were carrying guns and clubs. Four of them entered the mill while two more stood guard at the door, watching the road in both directions to shoo any traffic along while they did their business. One of the men standing by the road shouted encouragement through the door to the men who had entered the mill, and he banged on the wood siding of the mill with the axe handle he had with him. The other held a hunting rifle diagonally across his chest as though he was on guard duty.

The noise alerted Carolyn Sheffield, who came out on the porch of the store across the street and, seeing the commotion shouted at the robed figures, "You all get on out of here. That mill belongs to Mrs. Cordray, and you're trespassing."

One of the men shouted back to her at full volume, "Get your fat ass back in that store. This ain't none of your business. We ain't gonna be another Little Rock here in Calhoun County."

Across the street, Joyce went to call the sheriff. Cleo, who had gone inside with Joyce, set down the tray of glassware when she saw the Klan arrive, swung open the screen door, walked down the steps, and stepped tentatively into the yard. She walked slowly at first, then realizing how serious the situation was, moved faster and headed toward the mill. Carolyn, after calling the sheriff's office and leaving a message with one of the deputies, also began to move toward the mill.

The door opened, and four men came out dragging a bloody Sam Lloyd between them, carrying a shotgun and more clubs. Sam was unsteady, trying to get his legs to work between two beefy men. They were half dragging his feet as his legs tried to find purchase to walk.

Seeing this, Cleo began to run toward the men. As she neared the bridge, Cleo saw motion out of the corner of her eye and realized that John was coming back from his fishing trip in his boat. She screamed at him to hurry and help her.

She could hear the boat motor revving as John raced closer to the shore. She passed Wallace and Graham, who had been playing in the front of Mrs. Cordray's yard and were frozen still with fear and uncertainty. As she passed them, she shouted, "Go to Mrs. Cordray." Then, she began to run full tilt as the Klansmen dragged Sam toward their truck.

Now, one of the men outside the mill, seeing her fast approach, shouted at her. "Stay your ass back lady." To add emphasis, he pointed his rifle at her and adjusted the hood of the pillowcase so he could see better through the narrow eye slits. Cleo could tell, even from a distance, the head covering was small, like it was from a child's pillow, and although mostly white, had images of bunny rabbits scattered across the fabric. She had a strange thought that under other circumstances, this convoluted image would make her want to laugh.

John's boat hit the shore where he usually docked, and he pulled the pistol out of his tackle box as he rushed out to climb the small hill to the road. He tripped, fell and got back up, and continued to run as fast as he could.

Carolyn, after descending the porch steps of the store and moving slower in a run/walk, could see the complete picture of what was happening. When she saw John dock the boat and begin to run up the lawn and towards Cleo, she shouted, "Watch out, they got guns."

One of the Klansmen hustling Sam toward the truck, now feeling the pressure of white people coming to Sam's defense, shouted, "Let's finish this nigger and get out of here." Sam, hearing this threat, used his last bit of strength to struggle to get free. He fought and pulled at the two men holding to either side of him, throwing them off balance and making them lose their grip on his arms.

Cleo continued to run at the gang of men screaming at them. As she got nearer, almost there, Sam, now free from the hold of the men he had shrugged off, was hit on the head from behind with a devastating blow by another of the Klansmen with the axe handle he was holding. The blow stunned Sam and caused him to lurch forward. Sam grabbed wildly to steady himself, and he crashed into the man pointing the rifle at Cleo. The gun fired as she approached the group. Sam and the stunned Klansman fell and lay on the ground, spooning like lovers. Cleo crumpled to the ground.

John had just reached the road and was crossing the bridge when he saw both Sam, the Klansman, and Cleo go down. As he ran forward, he howled a primal scream and opened fire, pointing his pistol and squeezing the trigger repeatedly, aiming at the center of the bunch of robed figures who turned and ran toward the idling truck. One of the Klansmen was hit and fell. Three of the others picked him up and carried him to the bed of the truck. The man who had fallen with Sam shook him off, got up, and staggered to the truck as well. John continued to fire wildly as he ran until the gun was empty. They loaded the truck and roared off toward Morgan. As the truck left, one man shouted back, "We'll be back to get all you sons of bitches."

Carolyn, on her run from the store began to cross the bridge. Mrs. Cordray, back from her call to the sheriff and, hearing the gunshots, hobbled toward the street as fast as she dared using her cane while shouting at the boys to stay back. Graham and Wallace, who were still frozen in place, had watched everything from the front of the yard by the road.

162

John reached Sam and Cleo lying on the grass in front of the mill. A moment later, Carolyn reached Sam and turned the limp figure over as blood leaked from his head wound. "Oh honey, honey. What have they done? You poor thing."

John dropped to his knees next to Cleo. Her eyes and her mouth were still open in surprise, as though she could not quite figure out what had just happened. He leaned over her with his face filled with pain. As Carolyn tried to stem the blood from Sam's headwound with her skirt, she heard next to her a deep moan that slowly increased in volume into a shattering scream.

The Sheriff

The next day the sheriff of Calhoun County sat, talking with Joyce Cordray in her living room. He put his hat on the side table and had to adjust his gun holster to fit into the chair. "I wanted to give you a report on where things stand. They gonna take Sam over to the Phoebe Putney hospital in Albany. He might be safer over there, besides they ain't got much of a colored section in the Arlington hospital, and he needs some special treatment for his head. He's lucky that you are paying for him. He don't have any money to speak of or any insurance." He took a drink of the iced tea and sat the glass back near his hat. "They took the young lady's body over to the funeral home. If you don't know where to send her, I guess we need to bury her nearby. Maybe at the cemetery in Morgan."

Joyce shook her head. "I called my granddaughter up where she came from, and she can't find any family that Cleo had up there. I'd like to have her buried back out here. This was where she was most comfortable. This is where she came to escape that man in Boston. I can get John to dig her a grave. I think they became pretty good friends. I've seen her with him and the boys a time or two going fishing and such."

The sheriff used one of the arms of the chair to help him sit up taller. "Joyce, I'm real sorry about what happened over here." He let out a breath. "You know you got to be making some decisions."

164

"Bout what?"

"Bout John leaving."

"But he didn't do anything wrong. He was the one who run them off from what they were doing to Sam and killing Cleo. Why do you say he has to leave?"

"Cause I can't be over here from Morgan to protect him or you twenty-four hours a day. You know how the Klan works. Likely you know some of those boys under those hoods. I got my suspicions who they might have been. Went to talk to a couple of them. They had one fella with a gunshot and took him to the hospital, and all of them claimed it was a hunting accident. Not much I can do with four or five of them saying something, and we can't prove they was here. Even if we could prove they was here, by the time they finish telling their version of the story, it's gonna come out like Sam went crazy and shot a white lady, and they hit him to make him stop. Then John came along and started to help Sam by shooting at them ... at the white men. He hit one of those boys, likely the one they all are claiming was a hunting accident. So, I ain't got much to work with. That white boy's gonna make it. Still, that ain't gonna sit well with the Klan people."

He looked down at the floor and shuffled a foot back and forth. "Soon as they get enough liquor in them, they're likely to come here after John and maybe you too. They'll come after John's boys. Those little boys will catch it at school and in town and anywhere from all the other kids. The only way to avoid getting into something else is that John's gotta leave. If not, it's gonna come out bad for everybody. I don't have enough deputies to keep one here all the time. The only way for John to protect his family and you is for them to go away where nobody knows them or knows about what happened. Maybe someday things will change, and it'll get better, and they can come back. You need to talk to them and get them moving fast, before the Klan folk get all their buddies together and get some liquor in them. You know how these things go. Like I said, they'll say something like Sam started it and the shooing of Cleo was all his fault."

Joyce bowed her head in acknowledgment that what the sheriff was saying was likely to happen. She shook her head and started to say something about what a sorry excuse he was for a lawman when the sheriff continued.

"John needs to go today. I'll leave a deputy and a car here this afternoon, but if those Klan boys come over here tonight after John, they're likely to come for you too. I can protect you if he is gone, but It's too much to ask if he's still here."

True to his word, the sheriff left a deputy at Mrs. Cordray's house watching over everything that afternoon. After he had dug Cleo's grave, John changed the tag from his truck onto Cleo's car in the barn. He figured no one would recognize her car with a Georgia tag. Carolyn grabbed some food and supplies from the store to put in the back seat. John put whatever clothes and family photos, and trinkets he could get into bags and put them in the car with the boys. He then ran into the Cordray's guest house, grabbed a small bag from her closet, and put it in with their other clothes.

The Loot

Graham parked the rented camper truck on the side of the road across from where the mill used to be. He noticed that there were gaps in the rows of boards that had been part of the wall. The roof also showed missing patches, likely ripped off from the high winds during the frequent tornadoes in this part of the state.

Across the bridge, the fast-flowing stream spilled over the dam, still holding back the lake. The pavilion was gone. He heard it had burned not long after they left, and the swimming pool had been dismantled shortly after that. The store still seemed to be open but was in considerable disrepair and no longer featured gasoline pumps to attract visitors. There was no sign of Roscoe.

He had heard that after Mrs. Cordray's death, the family, who were still living far away, let Carolyn move into the house to look after things and collect the rent on the land they leased to nearby farmers. He smiled as he remembered the fascinating stories she used to tell him and Wallace.

Earlier, Graham had written a letter using his new name, which his father had changed when they left Georgia. With his real identity hidden, he asked permission to park where the remnants of the mill stood, and he inquired about renting a boat with a motor to do some fishing. He figured the self-contained camper with the fishing gear strapped to the sides would give him a place to stay, and he could be invisible if he avoided Carolyn. He'd keep away from her until he was ready. He watched her waddle across the road in the morning to open the store. Although older, heavier, and worn by time, she still wore the flowing, colorful blouses.

As he looked around at what had been the landscape of his childhood, he remembered Wallace and how much pleasure they had found here. How innocent they had been and ill-prepared for what the world would throw at them after they moved away. He looked over at the asphalt in the road at where the event took place, almost expecting to see the blood that had remained there until the next rain.

The threat from the Klan pushed them away from South Georgia to places where they knew no one, and their father's prospects for employment were even more limited. After the nest egg his father had retrieved from Cleo's home had run out, he and Wallace had to find ways to earn extra money to sustain them. As soon as he was old enough, his brother Wallace, who was more ashamed and embarrassed by their father's drinking, which had gotten worse every year, left home and joined the army. The escape from Cordray's Mill after the deaths of Cleo and the maiming of Sam had marked them all.

It was only after Wallace had been brought home from Vietnam and buried at the local cemetery with funds provided by the local American Legion that his father took his final nosedive into the booze. For the years before, since they had left Cordray's Mill, their father had been a silent drunk, brooding and morose, but thankfully not violent, although their lives had seemed even more isolated. Their friends from school did not want to come to their house, and they were not invited to spend the night at the homes of others. Unlike other families, they had no large family gatherings. They seemed to have nothing in common with the lives of other childhoods.

The boys grew up with the image of Cleo's death fixed in their minds. Graham could tell their father longed for Cleo, who had died in his arms. Many days he lay in bed hugging himself in a fetal position. For Graham, that bloody day was a recurring nightmare, with the images playing like a film in slow motion. Their father never wanted to discuss it, and the boys had to sneak to talk to each other about the incident that was the most powerful thing that had ever happened to them.

As his father's health was getting worse one afternoon and as Graham was sitting by his hospital bed, he told him the full story about Cleo. They had become lovers and had made plans to be together and raise the boys in a normal home. It was Cleo's secret money that was going to give them the ability to move away and start over. That was the secret Graham had come here to find.

When Cleo and John became close, she told him about the money and her fears, and his father had said, "I don't know nothing about all that, but if you want to hide a suitcase, I can help. Remember when I showed you that big cypress tree? That's my special secret fishing place. We'd need to get us a waterproof box that can be sealed so I can put it out there in the pond. We could put it on a chain tied to the tree and leave it in the water nearby. Nobody'd ever find it there, and we can go pull it up when you need it."

Graham motored the boat into the cove and tied up at the old cypress back in the slough, which in the intervening years had partially filled in with silt. There were more knees and weeds intruding on the space than he remembered. The area was, however, still lost by itself away from the main body of water. Safe.

The metal box his father had made to hold the suitcase was still intact. His father had been a good craftsman when he put his mind to it. For over fifteen years, the container had been lying there chained to the tree and sunk in the pool of water at his father's favorite fishing hole. Because it was bulky and heavy to move, after it was in the boat, he broke the seal and took out the suitcase. Still dry. Still intact. He let the metal box and chain sink back into the water to become a nest for the fish.

Later, when he opened it in the security of the camper, he was astonished at the amount of money still there. He recalled the story Cleo had shared with his father of her flight from Boston as he thumbed through all that cash. He thought about the years that had passed and what had happened during that time. He wondered if all the events that had shaped his family and the failure of Cordray's Mill could be traced back to this money. Certainly, Cleo's coming here was, and the effect she had on their family. Maybe the civil rights stuff and the Klan and Sam Lloyd getting hit would have happened anyway. All the money lying there couldn't change the past, but maybe it could help the future.

As he had promised his father, he counted out two separate batches from the suitcase, each of about ten percent of the money, and put them in sturdy bags. He found where Sam Lloyd's family was still living over in Shellman and had a short visit with him. Sam was still rather trim for being almost ninety years old, but the blow from the axe handle and the intervening years had left him unsteady on his feet. Still, Graham could feel the same gentle kindness from Sam he remembered from his childhood. As he gave him one of the bags, he advised him and his family to use the money to supplement whatever income they had and not to spend it quickly, and not to bring attention to themselves. He said his father had put them in his will, and some of this was money his father had won when he hit a jackpot in Las Vegas. He left, knowing that this much money would make a huge difference in their lives.

The next day when Carolyn walked from the house over to tend to the store, he went into the backyard. There, towards the edge near the woods, was the place where he used to come to dig for worms. Now it was a place for graves, and he saw lined up in a row the headstones for Cleo next to Joyce Cordray, and next to Joyce was her dog, Talmadge.

Graham sat down on the grass and remembered the night after the fair when all of them were on her porch nearby, and there was a cool breeze blowing in the quiet of the dark. She sat both him and Wallace down and talked to them like they were grownups. Their dad was there, but she was the one in charge. She talked about the rude man at the fair and told them that when they grew up, they needed to understand that being a man wasn't about bossing people around. It was about understanding and kindness, and fairness. No one had the right to dominate another person with meanness. They should be kind to everyone, no matter if they were rich or poor or black or white or whatever.

Their father just looked down at the floor while she talked, but they could tell that he agreed with what she was saying. He remembered her looking at him and Wallace with those green eyes and achingly beautiful face and getting them to pledge to be fair and caring. That was just before it all ended, and he had wished that night could have gone on forever or that he could go back there. He knew that for all those years after when life was too much for his father to handle, he had tried to do better, but for some people, it was just too hard.

Strange, when they left here, everyone around him was so anxious and afraid. Now in the soft morning light, the weight and the fear he had felt for many years was gone. He felt comfortable and secure sitting here on the grass.

Until ten days ago, he had been content to hold onto the secret his father told him as he was dying. He had a regular job that gave him enough income so that with his wife's salary, they both could live without worrying about being evicted from the two-bedroom apartment in a middle-class neighborhood in the Midwest. Graham had felt he could go on living as he had, and he felt that as long as he and his wife held onto their jobs, they would be all right. Then ten days ago, his wife told him she had lost her job and was pregnant.

As he sat there on the grass, he spoke to Cleo's grave about what he had been thinking on the journey to Georgia. "You would have liked my wife, and I told her about you. We're gonna have a baby next year. Now that I have your money, I'm gonna make sure that she and my kids are taken care of. But, I'm also gonna share a lot of this money with other people who need it. We're gonna invest some of it in something new called computers. I think if you and my dad knew what it was, you would have wanted to do that as well. Anyway, if she's a girl, we're gonna name her, Cleo."

He then walked over to the store to see Carolyn and told her that he had needed a day or two to reacclimate himself to Cordray's Mill and the memories he had there before revealing himself to her. She was inquisitive and a little suspicious of his intentions but basically bought his story. The bag of money he gave her helped. One of the last things Carolyn told him as he was leaving was, "As if the world ain't crazy enough, now a fella just up the road, a peanut farmer, is sayin he is going to run for President of the United States."

As he headed home, he imagined what kind of life his kids might have and what kind of father he planned to be. In addition to his coming child, his thoughts mostly centered on his wife, the kind of mother she would be, and the family they would have together. Like many stories with a hope for the future, this one ends with a woman.

END